continued . . .

EYE OF THE STORM ·
Also published as MIDNIGHT MAN
"Heart-stopping . . . spectacular and surprising."
—*Abilene Reporter-News*

"Razor-edged . . . will give you an adrenaline high. It's a winner."
—*Tulsa World*

ON DANGEROUS GROUND
"A whirlwind of action, with a hero who can out-Bond old James. It's told in the author's best style, with never a pause for breath." —*The New York Times Book Review*

"A powerhouse tale of action and adventure."
—*The Tampa Tribune-Times*

SHEBA
"When it comes to thriller writers, one name stands well above the crowd—Jack Higgins." —The Associated Press

THUNDER POINT
"Dramatic . . . authentic . . . one of the author's best."
—*The New York Times*

"A rollicking adventure that twists and turns."
—*The San Diego Union-Tribune*

GRAVEYARD SHIFT
"One-hundred-percent-proof adventure."
—*The New York Times*

Brought
In
Dead

Jack Higgins

BERKLEY BOOKS, NEW YORK

THE BERKLEY PUBLISHING GROUP
Published by the Penguin Group
Penguin Group (USA) Inc.
375 Hudson Street, New York, New York 10014, USA
Penguin Group (Canada), 10 Alcorn Avenue, Toronto, Ontario M4V 3B2, Canada
(a division of Pearson Penguin Canada Inc.)
Penguin Books Ltd., 80 Strand, London WC2R 0RL, England
Penguin Group Ireland, 25 St. Stephen's Green, Dublin 2, Ireland (a division of Penguin Books Ltd.)
Penguin Group (Australia), 250 Camberwell Road, Camberwell, Victoria 3124, Australia
(a division of Pearson Australia Group Pty. Ltd.)
Penguin Books India Pvt. Ltd., 11 Community Centre, Panchsheel Park, New Delhi—110 017, India
Penguin Group (NZ), Cnr. Airborne and Rosedale Roads, Albany, Auckland 1310, New Zealand
(a division of Pearson New Zealand Ltd.)
Penguin Books (South Africa) (Pty.) Ltd., 24 Sturdee Avenue, Rosebank, Johannesburg 2196,
South Africa

Penguin Books Ltd., Registered Offices: 80 Strand, London WC2R 0RL, England

This is a work of fiction. Names, characters, places, and incidents either are the product of the author's imagination or are used fictitiously, and any resemblance to actual persons, living or dead, business establishments, events, or locales is entirely coincidental.

BROUGHT IN DEAD

A Berkley Book / published by arrangement with the author

PRINTING HISTORY
John Long Limited edition / 1967
Berkley edition / December 2004

Copyright © 1967 by Harry Patterson.
Hell Is Always Today excerpt by Jack Higgins copyright © 2005 by Harry Patterson.
Cover illustration by Yuan Lee. Cover design by Steven Ferlauto.

For information address: The Berkley Publishing Group,
a division of Penguin Group (USA) Inc.,
375 Hudson Street, New York, New York 10014.

ISBN: 0-425-19933-9

BERKLEY®
Berkley Books are published by The Berkley Publishing Group,
a division of Penguin Group (USA) Inc.,
375 Hudson Street, New York, New York 10014.
BERKLEY is a registered trademark of Penguin Group (USA) Inc.
The "B" design is a trademark belonging to Penguin Group (USA) Inc.

PRINTED IN THE UNITED STATES OF AMERICA

10 9 8 7 6 5 4 3 2 1

For Dorothy Limón—a real fan.

CHAPTER 1

The girl was young and might have been pretty once, but not now. Her right eye was almost closed, the cheek mottled by livid bruises and her lips had been split by the same violent blow that had knocked out three teeth.

She hobbled painfully into the Line-Up room supported by a woman P.C., a pathetic, broken figure with a blanket over her shoulders to conceal the torn dress. Miller and Brady were sitting on a bench at the far end of the room and Brady saw her first. He tapped his companion on the shoulder and Miller stubbed out his cigarette and went to meet her.

He paused, noting her condition with a sort of

clinical detachment, and the girl shrank back slightly from the strange young man with the white face and the eyes that seemed to stare right through her like dark glass.

Detective Sergeant Nicholas Miller was tired—more tired than he had been in a long, long time. In the ten hours he had already spent on duty, he had served as investigating officer at two burglaries, a factory break-in and a closing-hours brawl outside a pub near the market in which a youth had been slashed so badly across the face that it was more than likely that he would lose his right eye. This had been followed almost immediately by a particularly vile case of child cruelty which had involved forcible entry, in company with an N.S.P.C.C. inspector, of a house near the docks where they had found three children huddled together like animals, almost naked, showing all the signs of advanced malnutrition, squatting in their own dirt in a windowless boxroom that stank like a pigsty.

And now this. Compassion did not come easily at five o'clock on a dark February morning, but there was fear on this girl's face and she had suffered enough. He smiled and his whole personality seemed to change and the warmth reached out to envelop her so that sudden, involuntary tears sprang to her eyes.

"It's all right," he said. "Everything's going to be fine. Another couple of minutes and it'll be all over." He turned to Detective Constable Brady. "Let's have them, Jack."

Brady nodded and pressed a red button on a small control panel on the wall. A hard white light illuminated a stage at the far end of the room and a moment later, a door opened and half a dozen men filed in followed by two constables who marshalled them in line.

Miller took the girl gently by the arm, but before he could speak, she started to tremble violently. She managed to raise her right hand, pointing at the prisoner who stood number one in line, a great ox of a man, his right cheek disfigured by a jagged scar. She tried to speak, something rattled in her throat and she collapsed against Miller in a dead faint.

He held her close against his chest and looked up at the stage. "Okay, Macek, let's be having you."

A thick-set, fourteen-stone Irishman with fists like rocks, Detective Constable Jack Brady had been a policeman for twenty-five years. A quarter of a century of dealing with human wickedness in all its forms, of walking daily in squalor and filth and a gradual erosion of the spirit had left him harsh and embittered, a hard, cruel man who believed in nothing. And then a curious thing had happened. Certain villains now serving collectively some twenty-five years in one of Her Majesty's Prisons had thrown him down a flight of stairs, breaking his leg in two places and fracturing his skull, later leaving him for dead in a back street.

Most men would have died, but not Jack Brady. The priest was called, the last rites administered and then the surgeons took over and the nurses and physio-therapists, and in three months he was back on duty with a barely perceptible limp in his left leg.

The same, but not the same. For one thing he was noticed to smile more readily. He was still a good tough cop, but now he seemed gifted with a new understanding. It was as if through suffering himself, he had learned compassion for others.

The girl painfully signed her name at the bottom of the typed statement sheet and he helped her to her feet and nodded to the woman P.C.

"You'll be all right now, love. It's all over."

The girl left, sobbing quietly, and Miller came in holding a teletype flimsy. "Don't waste too much sympathy on her, Jack. I've just heard from C.R.O. She's got a record. Four previous convictions including larceny, conspiracy to steal, breaking and entering and illegal possession of drugs. To cap that little lot, she's been on the trot from Peterhill Remand Home since November last year." He dropped the flimsy on the table in disgust. "We can certainly pick them."

"That still doesn't excuse what Macek did to her," Brady said. "Underneath that surface toughness she's just a frightened little girl."

"Sweetness and light." Miller said. "That's all I need." He yawned, reaching for a cigarette. The packet was empty and he crumpled it with a sigh. "It's been a long night."

Brady nodded, applying a match to the bowl of his pipe. "Soon be over."

The door opened and Macek entered, escorted by a young probationer constable. The Pole slumped down on one of the hard wooden chairs at the table and Miller turned to the probationer.

"I could do with some tea and a packet of cigarettes. See what the canteen can offer, will you?"

The young constable went on his way briskly, for Miller was a particular hero of his—Nick Miller, the man with the law degree who had made Detective Sergeant with only five years' service. All this and an interest, so it was rumoured, in his brother's business that enabled him to live in a style to which few police officers were accustomed.

As the door closed, Miller turned to Macek. "Now then, you bastard, let's get down to it."

"I've got nothing to say," Macek said woodenly.

Brady laughed harshly and there was a heavy silence. Macek looked furtively at Miller, who was examining his fingernails, and said desperately, "All right, so I knocked her around a little. Bloody little tart. She had it coming."

"Why?" Brady demanded.

"I took her in," Macek said. "Gave her a place to stay. The best of everything. Then I find her sneaking out at two in the morning with my wallet, my watch and everything else of value she could lay her hands on. What would you have done?"

He sounded genuinely aggrieved and Miller picked up the girl's statement. "She says here that you've been living together for five weeks."

Macek nodded eagerly. "I gave her the best—the best there was."

"What about the men?"

"What men?"

"The men you brought round to the house every night. The men who called because they needed a woman."

"Do me a favour," Macek said. "Do I look like a pimp?"

"Don't press me to answer that," Miller told him. "You've kept the girl under lock and key for the past two weeks. When she couldn't take any more, you beat her up and threw her out."

"You try proving that."

"I don't need to. You said you've been living together as man and wife."

"So what? It's a free country."

"She's just fifteen."

Macek's face turned grey. "She can't be."

"Oh, yes she can. We've got her record card."

Macek turned desperately to Brady. "She didn't tell me."

"It's a hard cruel world, isn't it, Macek?" Brady said.

The Pole seemed to pull himself together. "I want a lawyer."

"Are you going to make a statement?" Miller asked.

Macek glared across the table. "You get stuffed," he said viciously.

Miller nodded. "All right, Jack, take him down and book him. Make it abduction of a minor and rape. With any luck and his record, we might get him seven years."

Macek sat there staring at him, horror in his eyes, and Jack Brady's iron fist descended, jerking from the chair. "On your way, soldier."

Macek stumbled from the room and Miller turned to the window and pulled the curtain. Rain drifted across the glass in a fine spray and beyond, the first light of morning streaked the grey sky. The door opened behind him and the young probationer entered, the tea and cigarettes on a tray. "That'll be six bob, sarge."

Miller paid him and slipped the cigarettes into his pocket. "I've changed my mind about tea. You have it. I'm going home. Tell Detective Constable Brady I'll 'phone him this afternoon."

He walked along the quiet corridor, descended three flights of marble stairs and went out through the swing doors of the portico at the front of the Town Hall. His car was parked at the bottom of the steps with several others, a green Mini-Cooper, and he paused beside it to light a cigarette.

It was exactly five-thirty and the streets were strangely empty in the grey morning. The sensible thing to do was to go home to bed and yet he felt strangely restless. It was as if the city lay waiting for him and obeying a strange, irrational impulse he turned up the collar of his dark blue Swedish trench-coat against the rain and started across the square.

For some people the early morning is the best part of the day and George Hammond was one of these. Lockkeeper in charge of the great gates that pre-vented the canal from emptying itself into the river basin below, he had reported for duty at five-forty-five, rain or snow, for more than forty years. Walking through the quiet streets, he savoured the calm morn-ing with a conscious pleasure that never varied.

He paused at the top of the steps at the end of

the bridge over the river and looked down into the basin. They catered mainly for barge traffic this far upstream and they floated together beside the old Victorian docks like basking sharks.

He went down the steps and started along the bank. One section of the basin was crammed with coal barges offering a convenient short-cut to the other side and he started to work his way across.

He paused on the edge of the final barge, judging the gap between the thwart and the wharf. He started his jump, gave a shocked gasp and only just managed to regain his balance.

A woman stared up at him through the grey-green water. In a lifetime of working on the river George Hammond had found bodies in the basin before, but never one like this. The eyes stared past him, fixed on eternity, and for some inexplicable reason he knew fear.

He turned, worked his way back across the river, scrambled up on the wharf and ran along the bank.

Nick Miller had just started to cross the bridge as Hammond emerged from the top of the steps and leaned against the parapet sobbing for breath.

Miller moved forward quickly. "Anything wrong?"

"Police!" Hammond gasped. "I need the police."

"You've found them," Miller said crisply. "What's up?"

"Girl down there in the water," Hammond said. "Other side of the coal barges beneath the wharf."

"Dead?" Miller demanded.

Hammond nodded. "Gave me a hell of a turn, I can tell you."

"There's an all-night café on the other side of the bridge. 'Phone for a patrol car and an ambulance from there. I'll go down and see what I can do."

Hammond nodded, turned away and Miller went down the steps quickly and moved along the bank. It had stopped raining and a cool breeze lifted off the water so that he shivered slightly as he jumped for the deck of the first coal barge and started to work his way across.

He couldn't find her at first and then a sudden eddy of the current swirled, clearing the flotsam from the surface and she stared up at him.

And she was beautiful—more beautiful than he had ever known a woman to be, that was the strangest thing of all. The body had drifted into the arched entrance of a vault under the wharf and hung suspended just beneath the surface. The dress floated around her in a cloud as did the long golden hair and there was a look of faint surprise in the eyes, the lips parted slightly as if in wonder at how easy it had been.

Up on the bridge, there was the jangle of a patrol car's bell and in the distance, the siren of the approaching ambulance sounded faintly. But he couldn't wait. In some strange way this had become personal. He took off his trenchcoat and jacket, slipped off his shoes and lowered himself over the side.

The water was bitterly cold and yet he was hardly conscious of the fact as he swam into the archway. At that moment, the first rays of the morning sun broke through the clouds, striking into the water so that she seemed to smile as he reached under the surface and took her.

A line of broad steps dropped into the basin twenty yards to the right and he swam towards them, standing up when his knees bumped a shelving bank of gravel, lifting her in his arms.

But now she looked different. Now she looked dead. He stood there knee-deep, staring down at her, a lump in his throat, aware of a feeling of personal loss.

"Why?" he said to himself softly. "Why?"

But there was no answer, could never be and as the ambulance turned on the wharf above him he went up the steps slowly, the girl cradled in his arms so that she might have been a child sleeping.

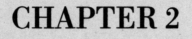

CHAPTER 2

Detective Superintendent Bruce Grant, head of the city's Central Division C.I.D., stood at the window of his office drinking a cup of tea and stared out morosely at the driving rain. He had a slight headache and his liver was acting up again. He was getting old, he decided—old and fat through lack of exercise and the stack of paperwork waiting on his desk didn't help. He lit a cigarette, his first of the day, sat down and started on the In-tray.

The first report was headed *Found Dead— Unidentified.* Grant read it through, a slight frown on his face, and pressed the button on his intercom.

"Is Sergeant Miller in?"

"I believe he's in the canteen, sir," a neutral voice replied.

"Get him for me, will you?"

Miller arrived five minutes later, immaculate in a dark blue worsted suit and freshly laundered white shirt. Only the skin that was stretched a little too tightly over the high cheekbones gave any hint of fatigue.

"I thought you were supposed to be having a rest day?" Grant said.

"So did I, but I'm due in court at ten when Macek is formally charged. I'm asking for a ten-day remand. That girl's going to be in hospital for at least a week."

Grant tapped the form on his desk, "I don't like the look of this one."

"The girl I pulled out of the river?"

"That's right. Are you certain there was no identification?"

Miller took an envelope from his pocket and produced a small gold medallion on the end of a slender chain. "This was around her neck."

Grant picked it up. "St. Christopher."

"Have a look on the back."

The engraving had been executed by an expert:

To Joanna from Daddy—1955. Grant looked up, frowning. "And this was all?"

Miller nodded. "She was wearing stockings, the usual in underclothes, and a reasonably expensive dress. One rather sinister point. Just beneath the maker's label there was obviously some sort of name tab. It's been torn out."

Grant sighed heavily. "Do you think she might have been put in?"

Miller shook his head. "Not a chance. There isn't a mark on her."

"Then it doesn't make sense," Grant said. "Suicide's an irrational act at the best of times. Are you asking me to accept that this girl was so cold-blooded about it that she took time off to try to conceal her identity?"

"It's the only thing that makes sense."

"Then what about the chain? Why didn't she get rid of that, too?"

"When you habitually wear a thing like that you tend to forget about it," Miller said. "Or maybe it meant a lot to her—especially as she was a Catholic."

"That's another thing—a Catholic committing suicide."

"It's been known."

"But not very often. There are times when such things as statistical returns and probability tables have their uses in this work—or didn't they teach you that at the staff college? What have Missing Persons got to offer?"

"Nothing yet," Miller said. "There's time of course. She looks old enough to have been out all night. Someone could conceivably wait for a day or two before reporting her missing."

"But you don't think so?"

"Do you?"

Grant looked at the form again and shook his head. "No, I'd say anything we're going to find out about this one, we'll have to dig up for ourselves."

"Can I have it?"

Grant nodded. "Autopsy isn't mandatory in these cases but I think I'll ask the County Coroner to authorise one. You never know what might turn up."

He reached for the 'phone and Miller went back into the main C.I.D. room and sat down at his desk. There was an hour to fill before his brief court appearance—a good opportunity to get rid of some of the paperwork in his In-tray.

For some reason he found it impossible to

concentrate. He leaned back in his chair, closing his eyes, and her face rose out of the darkness to meet him, still that faint look of surprise in the eyes, the lips slightly parted. It was as if she was about to speak, to tell him something but that was impossible.

God, but he was tired. He settled back in his chair and cat-napped, awaking at exactly five minutes to ten feeling curiously refreshed, but when he went down-stairs and crossed the square to the county court building, it wasn't the Macek case he was thinking about.

The City Mortuary was at the back of the Medical School, a large, ugly building in Victorian Gothic with stained glass windows by the entrance. Inside, it was dark and cool with green tiled walls and a strange aseptic smell that was vaguely unpleasant.

Jack Palmer, the Senior Technician, was sitting at his desk in the small glass office at the end of the corridor. He turned and grinned as Miller paused in the doorway.

"Don't tell me—let me guess."

"Anything for me?" Miller asked.

"Old Murray's handled it himself. Hasn't had

time to make out his report yet, but he'll be able to tell you what you need to know. He's cleaning up now."

Miller peered through the glass wall into the white tiled hall outside the theatre and saw the tall, spare form of the University Professor of Pathology emerge from the theatre, the front of his white gown stained with blood.

"Can I go in?"

Palmer nodded. "Help yourself."

Professor Murray had removed his gown and was standing at the sluice, washing his hands and arms, when Miller entered. He smiled, speaking with the faint Scots accent of his youth that he had never been able to lose.

"Hardly the time of year to go swimming, especially in that open sewer we call a river. I trust you've been given suitable injections?"

"If I start feeling ill I'll call no one but you," Miller said, "that's a promise."

Murray reached for a towel and started to dry his arms. "They tell me you don't know who the girl is?"

"That's right. Of course she may be reported missing by someone within the next day or two."

"But you don't think so? May I ask why?"

"It's not the usual kind of suicide. The pattern's all wrong. For one thing, the indications are that she did everything possible to conceal her identity before killing herself." He hesitated. "There's no chance that she was dumped, is there? Drugged beforehand or something like that?"

Murray shook his head. "Impossible—the eyes were still open. It's funny you should mention drugs though."

"Why?"

"I'll show you."

It was cold in the theatre and the heavy antiseptic smell could not wholly smother the sickly-sweet stench of death. Her body lay on the slab in the centre of the room covered with a rubber sheet. Murray raised the edge and lifted the left arm.

"Take a look."

The marks of the needle were plainly visible and Miller frowned. "She was a junkie?"

Murray nodded. "My tests indicate that she had an injection consisting of two grains of heroin and one of cocaine approximately half an hour before she died."

"And when would you say that was?"

"Let's see now. You pulled her out just before six, didn't you? I'd say she'd been in the water about five hours."

"Which means she went in at one a.m."

"Or thereabouts. One can't be exact. It was a cold night."

"Anything else?"

"What can I tell you? She was about nineteen, well nurtured. I'd say she'd been raised in more than comfortable surroundings."

"Was she a virgin?"

"Anything but—two months pregnant." He shook his head and added dryly. "A young woman very well acquainted with the sexual act."

"What about her clothes?"

"A chap was here from your Forensic Department. He took them away along with the usual things. Scrapings from under the fingernails, hair samples and so on."

Miller moved to the other side of the slab, hesitated and then pulled back the rubber sheet revealing the face. Murray had closed the eyes and she looked calm and peaceful, the skin smooth and colourless.

Murray covered her again gently, his face sombre.

"I think she was someone who had suffered a great deal. Too much for one so young."

Miller nodded, unable to speak. That strange aching dryness clutched at his throat again and he turned away quickly. As he reached the door, Murray called softly, "Nick!" Miller turned. "Keep me posted."

"I'll do that," Miller said and the rubber doors swung together behind him.

As he went out into the pale morning sunshine, Jack Brady crossed the car park to meet him.

"Grant thought you might need some help on this one. Have they finished the autopsy?"

Miller nodded. "Murray says she went into the river somewhere around one a.m. She was pregnant, by the way."

Brady nodded calmly. "Anything else?"

"She was a junkie. Heroin and cocaine."

"That should give us a lead." Brady took a buff envelope from his overcoat pocket. "I've checked with Forensic. They'll have a report ready by noon. These are from Photography."

Miller opened the envelope and examined the prints it contained. Those photography boys certainly knew their job. She might almost have been alive, an illusion helped by the fact that the photos had been taken before Murray had closed her eyes.

Brady took one and frowned. "A damned shame. She looks like a nice kid."

"Don't they always?" Miller slipped the other prints into his pocket. "I think I'll go and see Dr. Das. He knows just about every junkie in town."

"What about me?"

Miller took the gold St. Christopher from his breast pocket and handed it over. "You're a good Catholic, aren't you, Jack?"

"I go to Mass now and then."

"Maybe the girl did. There's an inscription on the other side. Work your way round the parish priests. Someone may recognise her photo or even the medal."

"More shoe leather," Brady groaned.

"Good for your soul this one. I'll drop you off at the Cathedral if you like."

They got into the car and Brady glanced at his copy of the girl's photograph again before putting it away in his wallet. He shook his head. "It doesn't make sense, does it? Have you any idea what it's like down there on the docks at that time in the morning?"

"Just about the darkest and loneliest place in the world," Miller said.

Brady nodded. "One thing's certain. She must have been pretty desperate. I'd like to know what got her into that state."

"So would I, Jack," Miller said. "So would I," and he released the handbrake and drove rapidly away.

Drug addicts are possibly the most difficult of all patients to handle and yet Dr. Lal Das specialised in them. He was a tall cadaverous Indian, with an international reputation in the field, who persisted in running a general practice in one of the less salubrious parts of the city, a twilight area of tall, decaying Victorian houses.

He had just finished his morning calls and was having coffee in front of the surgery fire when Miller was shown in. Das smiled and waved him to a seat. "A pleasant surprise. You will join me?"

"Thanks very much."

Das went to the sideboard and returned with another cup. "A social call?"

"I'm afraid not." Miller produced one of the photos. "Have you ever seen her before?"

Das shook his head. "Who is she?"

"We don't know. I pulled her out of the river this morning."

"Suicide?"

Miller nodded. "Professor Murray did an autopsy. She'd had a fix about half an hour before she died."

"What was the dosage?"

"Two grains of heroin—one of cocaine."

"Then she can't have been an addict for long. Most of my regulars are on five, six or seven grains of heroin alone. There were the usual tracks in her arm?"

"Only a few."

"Which would seem to confirm my theory." Das sighed. "What a tragedy. She looks such a pleasant child." He handed the photo back. "I'm sorry, I can't help. You have no idea as to her identity at all?"

"I was hoping she might be a registered addict."

Das shook his head emphatically. "Definitely not. We have a new scheme operating under which all registered addicts must attend my clinic at St. Gregory's Hospital on Saturday mornings."

"Is this as well as their visits to their own doctor?"

Das nodded. "Believe me, sergeant, if she was registered I would know her."

Miller swallowed the rest of his coffee. "I'd better get moving. Got a lot of ground to cover."

"Why not have a chat with Chuck Lazer?" Das said. "If anyone could help, he could."

"That's an idea," Miller said. "How is he these days? Still dry?"

"For ten months now. A remarkable achievement, especially when one considers that his intake was of the order of seven grains of heroin and six of cocaine daily."

"I hear he's running a small casino club now."

"Yes, the Berkley in Cork Square. Very exclusive. Haven't you been?"

"I got an invitation to the opening, but I couldn't make it. Does he still play a good jazz piano?"

"Oscar Peterson at his best couldn't improve on him. I was there last Saturday. We were talking about you."

"I'll drop in and see him," Miller said. "Where's he living now?"

"He has an apartment over the club. Very pleasant. He'll probably be in bed now, mind you."

"I'll take that chance."

They went out into the hall. Das opened the front

door and shook hands formally. "If I can help in any way . . ."

"I'll let you know," Miller said and he ran down the steps to the Mini-Cooper and drove away.

Cork Square was a green lung in the heart of the city, a few sycamore trees scattered here and there, the whole surrounded by quiet, grey-stone Georgian houses, most of them occupied by consultant physicians and barristers.

The entrance to the Berkley Club was a cream-painted door, its brass handle and plate shining in the sunlight. Even the neon sign was in perfect taste with the surroundings and had obviously been specially designed. Miller pulled in to the kerb, got out and looked up at the front of the building.

"Hey, Nick, you old so-and-so! What gives?"

The cry echoed across the square and as he turned, Chuck Lazer moved out of the trees, a couple of Dalmatians straining ahead of him on twin leads. Miller went to meet him, leaving the path and crossing the damp grass.

"Hello there, Chuck. What's all this?" He bent down to pat the eager dogs.

The American grinned. "Part of my new image. The customers love it. Gives the place tone. But never mind that. How are you? It's been too long."

He was bubbling over with genuine pleasure, the blue eyes sparkling. When Miller had first met him almost a year previously during a murder investigation, Lazer had been hopelessly hooked on heroin with the gaunt fleshless face of an emaciated saint. Now, there was meat on his bones and the neatly trimmed dark fringe beard combined with the expensive sports coat to give him a positively elegant appearance.

He slipped the dogs' leads and the Dalmatians moved into the flower beds as he and Miller sat down on a bench.

"I've just seen Das. He told me he'd been to the club. Gave me a glowing report." Miller offered him a cigarette. "On you too."

Lazer grinned. "No need to worry about me, Nick. I'd cut my throat before I'd take another shot." He lit his cigarette and exhaled smoke in a blue cloud. "What did you want with Das—business?"

Miller produced one of the photos and passed it across. "Know her?"

Lazer shook his head. "Can't say I do." He

frowned suddenly. "Heh, isn't that a morgue photograph?"

Miller nodded. "I pulled her out of the river this morning. Trouble is we can't identify her."

"Suicide?"

"That's right. The autopsy showed she was an addict. I was hoping she might be registered, that Das might know her."

"And she isn't? That makes it difficult."

"What's the drug market like now, Chuck?" Miller said. "Where would she get the stuff?"

"Difficult to say. I've been out of circulation for quite a while, remember. As far as I know, there isn't any really organised peddling if that's what you mean. Remember where you first met me."

Miller grinned. "Outside the all-night chemist's in City Square."

"That's where it changes hands. Most registered addicts see their doctor at his evening surgery and usually get a prescription dated for the following day. Legally, they can have it filled from midnight onwards which is why you always find a bunch waiting in the all-night chemist's in any big city round about that time. The non-registered users hang around outside hoping to buy a few pills.

They're usually in luck. Quite a few doctors tend to over-prescribe."

"So all I have to do is go down to City Square at midnight and pass her photo around?"

"If she was an addict, someone will recognise her, that's for sure. The most exclusive club in the world."

"Thanks very much," Miller said. "I didn't get any sleep last night either."

"You shouldn't have joined." Lazer chuckled and then his smile faded.

Miller glanced across to the club as a dark blue Rolls eased in to the kerb. The first man to emerge was built like a pro wrestler, shoulders bulging massively under a dark blue overcoat. The driver came round to join him, a small, wiry man with jet black hair, and held open the rear door.

The man who got out was large and rather fleshy with hair so pale that it was almost white. He wore a single-breasted suit of dark grey flannel that was straight out of Savile Row, a white gardenia in the buttonhole, and carried himself with the habitual arrogance of a man who believes that he exists by a kind of divine right. The small man said something to him and they all turned and glanced at Lazer and Miller.

"Friends of yours?" Miller said as they moved across the grass.

Lazer shook his head. "I wouldn't say that exactly. The fancy boy is Max Vernon. Came up from London about four months ago and bought out Harry Faulkner. Took over his betting shops, the Flamingo Club—everything."

"What about his minders?"

"The big boy's called Carver—Simon Carver. The little guy's the one to watch. Stratton—I don't know his first name."

"Have they been leaning on you?"

Lazer bared his teeth in a mirthless grin. "Nothing quite so obvious. Let's say I've got a very nice little business and Mr. Vernon would like a piece of the action. For a consideration, of course. All nice and legal. Unfortunately, I'm not interested in selling."

Vernon paused a couple of yards away, Carver and Stratton on either side of him. "Hello there, old man," he said cheerfully. "I was hoping to find you in. Time we had another little chat."

"Not in my book it isn't," Lazer replied.

Carver took a step forward, but before anything could develop, Miller said quickly, "That's an Old Etonian tie you're wearing, did you know that?"

Vernon turned, his smile still hooked firmly into place. "How very gratifying. You're the first person to recognise it since I've been here. Of course, we are a little far north."

"Dangerous country," Miller said. "We've been known to roll boulders down the hillside on unwary travellers—stone strangers."

"How fascinating." Vernon turned to Lazer. "Introduce me to your friend, Chuck."

"A pleasure," Lazer said. "Nick Miller. Detective Sergeant, Central C.I.D."

Vernon hesitated momentarily and then extended his hand. "Always a pleasure to meet the law."

Miller stayed where he was on the bench, hands tucked casually into his pockets. "I can't say it's mutual."

"You watch your mouth, copper," Carver said harshly.

He started to move, Lazer whistled twice and the Dalmatians arrived on the run. They stood beside him, pointing at Carver, something rumbling deep down in their throats.

Carver hesitated, obviously uncertain, and Miller laughed. "Know why they call them carriage dogs, Carver? They were specially bred during the eighteenth century as travelling companions to take care of highwaymen."

Something glowed deep in Carver's eyes and Vernon chuckled. "That's damned good. Damned good." He grinned at Carver. "See, you learn something new every day of the week."

He turned away without another word and walked back to the Rolls, Carver and Stratton hurrying after him. Lazer leaned down to fondle the ears of the two dogs and Miller said softly, "I think you could have trouble there, Chuck."

"If it comes, I'll handle it."

Miller shook his head. "You mean I'll handle it and that's an order." He got to his feet and grinned. "I've got to get moving."

Lazer stood up and produced a small gold-edged card from his breast pocket. "I know it's illegal to do it this way, but there's a membership card. Why not drop in? It's been a long time since I heard you play piano."

"I might just do that," Miller said and he turned and walked away across the grass.

As the Rolls-Royce moved out into the main traffic stream, Max Vernon leaned forward and slid back the glass panel of the partition.

"This chap Miller," he said to Carver, "know anything about him?"

"Not a thing."

"Then start digging. I want to know everything—everything there is to know."

"Any special reason?" Carver said.

"Well, let me put it this way. The only other copper I've ever met who made a practice of wearing sixty-guinea suits is doing a five stretch in the Ville for corruption."

Carver's eyes widened and Vernon closed the glass panel, leaned back in his seat and lit a cigarette, a slight smile on his face.

CHAPTER 3

Henry Wade was fat and balding and his several chins and horn-rimmed spectacles gave him the deceptively benign air of a prosperous publican or back street bookie. He was neither. He was head of the department's Forensic section with the rank of Detective Inspector and the ready smile concealed a brain that in action had the cutting edge of a razor.

When Miller went into the small office at one end of the police lab, he found Wade at his desk filling in a report, covering the paper with the neat italic script that was his special pride.

He turned and smiled. "Hello, Nick, I was wondering when you'd turn up."

"Anything for me?"

"Not much, I'm afraid. Come on. I'll show you."

Miller followed him into the lab., nodding to the bench technicians as he passed. The girl's clothing was laid out neatly on a table by the window.

Wade went through the items one by one. "The stockings are a well-known brand sold everywhere and the underwear she bought at Marks & Spencer's along with just about every other girl in the country these days."

"What about the dress?"

"Reasonably expensive, but once again, a well-known brand name available at dozens of shops and stores. One interesting point. Just below the maker's label, a name tab's been torn out."

He picked up the dress pointing with a pair of tweezers and Miller nodded. "I noticed."

"I had a hunch about that. We matched up a piece of the tab that was still attached to the dress and my hunch paid off. It's a Cash label. You must have seen them. Little white tabs with the individual's name woven in red. People buy them for schoolchildren or students going away to college."

Miller nodded. "Thousands of people, including my sister-in-law. Her two kids have them sewn into just about every damned thing they own. Is that all?"

"No—one other thing. When we checked the nail scrapings we discovered a minute quantity of oil paint. There were one or two spots on the dress, too."

"An artist?" Miller said. "That's something."

"Don't be too certain. Lots of people do a little painting these days." Henry Wade grinned and slapped him on the shoulder. "You shouldn't have joined, Nick lad. You shouldn't have joined."

Grant was still working away at his desk when Miller peered round the door. "Got a minute?"

"Just about." Grant sat back and lit a cigarette. "How's it going?"

"So far, not so good, but it was something else I wanted to mention. What do you know about a man called Vernon?"

"Max Vernon, the bloke from London who took over Faulkner's casino and betting shops?" Grant shrugged. "Not much. The Chief introduced him to me at the Conservative Ball. Obviously a gentleman. Public school and all that sort of thing."

"Right down to his Old Etonian tie." Miller

suppressed a strong desire to burst into laughter. "He's leaning on Chuck Lazer."

"He's what?" Grant said incredulously.

"It's true enough," Miller said. "I was chatting to Lazer in the Square outside his place when Vernon turned up with a couple of heavies named Carver and Stratton. No comic Vaudeville act those two, believe me. Vernon wants a piece of the Berkley Club. He'll pay for it of course, all nice and legal, but Chuck Lazer better play ball or else . . ."

Grant was a different man as he flicked one of the switches on his intercom. "Records? Get on to C.R.O. in London at once. I want everything they've got on Max Vernon and two men now working for him called Carver and Stratton. Top priority."

He turned back to Miller. "What happened?"

"Nothing much. Vernon didn't say anything in the slightest way incriminating. On the face of it, he's making a perfectly legitimate business offer."

"Did he know who you were?"

"Not until Lazer introduced us."

Grant got up and walked to the window. "I don't like the sound of this at all."

"It certainly raises interesting possibilities," Miller said. "Those houses Faulkner was running in

Gascoigne Square. His call-girl racket. Has Vernon taken those over too?"

"An intriguing thought." Grant sighed heavily. "It never rains but it pours. Try and look in this afternoon at about three. I should have heard from C.R.O. by then."

When Miller went back into the main C.I.D. room a young P.C. was hovering beside his desk. "I took a message for you while you were in with the super, sergeant."

"Who from?"

"Jack Brady. He said he was ringing from St. Gemma's Roman Catholic Church in Walthamgate. He'd like you to join him there as soon as you can."

"Anything else?"

"Yes—he said to tell you that he thinks he's traced the girl."

The lights in the little church were very dim and down by the altar the candles flickered and the figure of the Virgin in the chapel to one side seemed to float there in the darkness.

For Miller, this was unfamiliar territory and he paused, waiting as Jack Brady dipped a knee, crossing himself reverently. The man they had come to see knelt in prayer at the altar and when he got to his feet and came towards them, Miller saw that he was very old, the hair silvery in the subdued light.

Brady made the introductions. "Father Ryan, this is Detective Sergeant Nick Miller."

The old man smiled and took Miller's hand in a grip that was surprisingly firm. "Jack and I are old friends, sergeant. For fifteen years or more he ran the boxing team for me at the Dockside Mission boys' club. Shall we sit in the porch? A pity to miss the sunshine. It's been a hard winter."

Brady opened the door and Father Ryan preceded them. He sat on the polished wooden bench that overlooked the quiet graveyard with the row of cypress trees lining the road beyond the high wall.

"I understand you might be able to help us with our enquiry, Father," Miller said.

The old man nodded. "Could I see the photo again?"

Miller passed it across and for a moment there was silence as Father Ryan examined it. He sighed heavily. "Poor girl. Poor wee girl."

"You know her?"

"She called herself Joanna Martin."

"Called herself . . . ?"

"That's right. I don't think it was her real name."

"Might I ask why?"

Father Ryan smiled faintly. "Like you, I deal with people, sergeant. Human beings in the raw. Let's say one develops an instinct."

Miller nodded. "I know what you mean."

"She first came to my church about three months ago. I noticed something different about her at once. This is a twilight area, most of the houses in multiple occupation, the tenants constantly coming and going. Joanna was obviously the product of a safer more ordered world. She was out of her element."

"Can you tell us where she lived?"

"She had a room with a Mrs. Kilroy, a parishioner of mine. It's not far from here. I've given Detective Constable Brady the address."

Somehow, the fact that he had used Brady's official title seemed to underline a new formality in the interchange. It was as if he were preparing himself for the question that he knew must come.

"I know this must be a difficult situation for you, Father," Miller said gently. "But this girl had

49

problems and they must have been pretty desperate to make her take the way out that she did. Can you throw any light on them?"

Brady cleared his throat awkwardly and shuffled his feet. The old man shook his head. "For me, the secrecy of the confessional must be absolute. Surely you must be aware of that, sergeant."

Miller nodded. "Of course, Father. I won't press you any further. You've already helped us a great deal."

Father Ryan stood up and held out his hand. "If I can help in any other way, don't hesitate to get in touch."

Brady was already moving away. Miller started to follow and hesitated. "One more thing, Father. I understand there could be some difficulty regarding burial because of the manner of death."

"Not in this case," Father Ryan said firmly. "There are several mitigating circumstances. I intend raising the matter with the Bishop personally. I may say with some certainty that I foresee little difficulty."

Miller smiled. "I'm glad."

"Forgive me for saying so, but you appear to have some personal interest here? May I ask why?"

"I pulled her out of the river myself," Miller told

him. "Something I'm not likely to forget in a hurry. I know one thing—I'd like to get my hands on whoever was responsible."

Father Ryan sighed. "It's a strange thing, but in spite of the fact that most people believe priests to be somehow cut off from the real world, I come face to face with more human wickedness in a week than the average man does in a lifetime." He smiled gently. "And I still believe that at heart, most human beings are good."

"I wish I could agree, Father," Miller said sombrely. "I wish I could agree." He turned and walked away quickly to where Jack Brady waited at the gate.

Mrs. Kilroy was a large, unlovely widow with flaming red hair that had come straight out of a bottle and a thin mouth enlarged by orange lipstick into an obscene gash.

"I keep a respectable place here, I've never had any trouble before," she said as she led the way upstairs.

"No trouble, Mrs. Kilroy," Brady said persuasively. "We just want to see the room, that's all, and ask a few questions."

The landing was long and dark, its polished lino covered by a thin strip of worn carpeting. The door at the far end was locked. She produced a bunch of keys, opened it and led the way in.

The room was surprisingly large and furnished in Victorian mahogany. The curtains at the only window were partially closed, the traffic sounds outside muted and unreal as if from another world and a thin bar of sunlight fell across the floor adding a new richness to the faded colours of the old Indian carpet.

It was the neatness that was so surprising and the cleanliness. The bed had been stripped, the blankets folded into squares and stacked at one end of the mattress and the top of the dressing table had quite obviously been dusted. Miller opened one or two of the empty drawers, closed them again and turned.

"And this is exactly how you found the room this morning?"

Mrs. Kilroy nodded. "She came and knocked on my door last night at about ten o'clock."

"Had she been out?"

"I wouldn't know. She told me she'd be moving today."

"Did she say why?"

Mrs. Kilroy shook her head. "I didn't ask. I was more interested in getting a week's rent in lieu of notice, which was the agreement."

"And she paid?"

"Without a murmur. Mind you there was never any trouble over her rent, I'll say that. Not like some."

Brady had busied himself during the conversation in moving around the room, checking all drawers and cupboards. Now he turned and shook his head. "Clean as a whistle."

"Which means that when she left, she must have taken everything with her." Miller turned to Mrs. Kilroy. "Did you see her go?"

"Last time I saw her was about half ten. She knocked on the door and told me she'd some rubbish to burn. Asked if she could put it in the central heating furnace in the cellar."

"Have you been down there since?"

"No need. It has an automatic stoking system. Only needs checking every two days."

"I see." Miller walked across to the window and pulled back the curtains. "Let's go back to when you last saw her. Did she seem worried or agitated?"

Mrs. Kilroy shook her head quickly. "She was just the same as she always was."

"And yet she killed herself less than three hours later."

"God have mercy on her." There was genuine

horror in Mrs. Kilroy's voice and she crossed herself quickly.

"What else can you tell me about her? I understand she'd been a tenant of yours for about three months."

"That's right. She arrived on the doorstep one afternoon with a couple of suitcases. As it happened, I had a vacancy and she offered a month's rent in advance in lieu of references."

"What did you think of her?"

Mrs. Kilroy shrugged. "She didn't really fit in. Too much of the lady for a district like this. I never asked questions, I always mind my own business, but if anyone had a story to tell it was her."

"Father Ryan doesn't seem to think Joanna Martin was her real name."

"I shouldn't be surprised."

"What did she do for a living?"

"She paid her rent on time and never caused any trouble. Whatever she did was her own business. One thing—she had an easel set up in here. Used to paint in oils. I once asked her if she was a student, but she said it was only a hobby."

"Did she go out much—at night, for instance?"

"She could have been out all night and every

night as far as I was concerned. All my lodgers have their own keys." She shrugged. "More often than not I'm out myself."

"Did anyone ever call for her?"

"Not that I noticed. She kept herself to herself. The only outstanding thing I do remember is that sometimes she looked really ill. I had to help her up the stairs one day. I wanted to call the doctor, but she said it was just her monthly. I saw her later that afternoon and she looked fine."

Which was how one would expect her to look after a shot of heroin and Miller sighed. "Anything else?"

"I don't think so," Mrs. Kilroy hesitated. "If she had a friend at all, it was the girl in number four—Monica Grey."

"Why do you say that?"

"I've seen them going out together, mainly in the afternoons."

"Is she in now?"

"Should be. As far as I know, she works nights in one of these gaming clubs."

Miller turned to Brady. "I'll have a word with her. You get Mrs. Kilroy to show you where the furnace is. See what you can find."

The door closed behind them and Miller stood there in the quiet, listening. But there was nothing here—this room had no personality. It was as if she had never been here at all and after all, what did he really know about her? At the moment she existed only as a series of apparently contradictory facts. A well-bred girl, she had come down to living in a place like this. A sincere Catholic, she had committed suicide. Educated and intelligent, but also a drug addict.

None of it made any sense at all and he went along the corridor and knocked at number four. There was an immediate reply and he opened the door and entered.

She was standing in front of the dressing table, her back to the door and dressed, as far as he could judge in that first moment, in stockings and a pair of dark briefs. In the mirror, he was aware of her breasts, high and firm, and then her eyes widened.

"I thought it was Mrs. Kilroy."

Miller stepped back into the corridor smartly, closing the door. A moment later it opened again and she stood there laughing at him, an old nylon housecoat belted around her waist.

"Shall we try again?"

Her voice was hoarse but not unattractive with a slight Liverpool accent and she had a turned-up nose that gave her a rather gamin charm.

"Miss Grey?" Miller produced his warrant card. "Detective Sergeant Miller—Central C.I.D. I wonder if I might have a word with you?"

Her smile slipped fractionally and a shadow seemed to cross her eyes as she stepped back and motioned him in. "What have I done now? Over-parked or something?"

There were times when the direct approach produced the best results and Miller tried it now. "I'm making enquiries into the death of Joanna Martin. I understand you might be able to help me."

It had the effect of a physical blow. She seemed to stagger slightly, then turned, groped for the end of the bed and sank down.

"I believe you were pretty good friends," Miller continued.

She stared up at him blindly then suddenly got to her feet, pushed him out of the way and ran for the bathroom. He stood there, a slight frown on his face and there was a knock on the outside door. He opened it to find Jack Brady waiting.

"Any luck?" Miller asked.

Brady held up an old canvas bag. "I found all sorts in the ash-pan. What about this for instance?"

He produced a triangular piece of metal, blackened and twisted by the fire, and Miller frowned. "This is a corner piece off a suitcase."

"That's right," Brady shook the bag in his right hand. "If the bits and pieces in here are anything to go by, I'd say she must have put every damned thing she owned into that furnace."

"Including her suitcase? She certainly wasn't leaving anything to chance." Miller sighed. "All right, Jack. Take that little lot down to the car and put in a call to H.Q. See if they've anything for us. I shan't be long."

He lit a cigarette, moved to the window and looked out into the back garden. Behind him the bathroom door opened and Monica Grey emerged.

She looked a lot brighter as she came forward and sat on the edge of the bed. "Sorry about that. It was rather a shock. Joanna was a nice kid." She hesitated and then continued. "How—how did it happen?"

"She jumped in the river." Miller gave her a cigarette and lit it for her. "Mrs. Kilroy tells me you were good friends."

Monica Grey took the smoke deep into her lungs and exhaled with a sigh of pleasure. "I wouldn't say that exactly. I went to the cinema with her sometimes in the afternoons or she came in for a coffee, mainly because she happened to live next door."

"You never went out with her at any other time?"

"I couldn't—I work nights. I'm a croupier at a gaming club in Gascoigne Square—the Flamingo."

"Max Vernon's place?"

She nodded. "Have you been there?"

"A long time ago. Tell me about Joanna? Where did she come from?"

Monica Grey shook her head. "She never discussed her past. She always seemed to live entirely in the present."

"What did she do for a living?"

"Nothing as far as I could tell. She spent a lot of time painting, but only as a hobby. I know one thing—she was never short of money."

"What about boy friends?"

"As far as I know, she didn't have any."

"Didn't that seem strange to you? She was an attractive girl."

"That's true, but she had her problems." She

appeared to hesitate and then went on. "If you've seen her body you must know what I'm getting at. She was a junkie."

"How did you know that?"

"I went into her room to borrow a pair of stockings one day and found her giving herself a shot. She asked me to keep quiet about it."

"Which you did?"

Monica Grey shrugged. "None of my affair how she got her kicks. It was one hell of a shame, but there was nothing I could do about it."

"She was a Catholic," Miller said, "did you know that?"

She nodded. "She went to church nearly every day."

"And yet she killed herself after burning everything she owned in the central heating furnace downstairs and ripping the name tab out of the dress she was wearing when she died. It's only by chance that we've managed to trace her this far and when we do, nobody seems to know anything about her. Wouldn't you say that was peculiar?"

"She was a strange kid. You could never tell what was going on beneath the surface."

"Father Ryan doesn't seem to think that Joanna Martin was her real name."

"If that's true, she certainly never gave me any clue."

Miller nodded, turned and paced across the room. He paused suddenly. The table against the wall was littered with sketches, mainly fashion drawings, some in pen and ink, others colour-washed. All showed indications of real talent.

"Yours?" he said.

Monica Grey stood up and walked across. "That's right. Like them?"

"Very much. Did you go to the College of Art?"

"For two years. That's what brought me here in the first place."

"What made you give it up?"

She grinned. "Forty quid a week at the Flamingo plus a dress allowance."

"Attractive alternative." Miller dropped the sketch he was holding. "Well, I don't think I need bother you any more." He walked to the door, paused and turned. "Just one thing. You do understand that if I can't trace her family, I may have to ask you to make the formal identification?"

She stood there staring at him, her face very white, and he closed the door and went downstairs. There was a pay 'phone fixed to the wall by the door and Brady leaned beside it filling his pipe.

He glanced up quickly. "Any joy?"

"Not really, but I've a feeling we'll be seeing her again."

"I got through to H.Q. There was a message for you from Chuck Lazer. Apparently he's been passing round the copy of the photo you gave him. He's come up with a registered addict who sold her a couple of pills outside the all-night chemist's in City Square just after midnight. If you guarantee no charge, he's agreed to make a statement."

"That's all right by me," Miller said. "You handle it, will you? I'll drop you off at Cork Square and you can go and see Chuck right away. I've a 'phone call to make first."

"Anything special?"

"Just a hunch. The girl liked to paint, we've established that. Another thing—that name tab she ripped out of her dress was a type commonly bought by students. I'm wondering if there might be a connection."

He found the number he wanted and dialled

quickly. The receiver was picked up almost at once at the other end and a woman's voice said, "College of Art."

"Put me through to the registrar's office please."

There was a momentary delay and then a pleasant Scottish voice cut in, "Henderson here."

"Central C.I.D. Detective Sergeant Miller. I'm making enquiries concerning a girl named Joanna Martin and I've good reason to believe she might have been a student at your college during the last couple of years. Would it take you long to check?"

"No more than thirty seconds, sergeant," Henderson said crisply. "We've a very comprehensive filing system." A moment later he was back. "Sorry, no student of that name. I could go back further if you like."

"No point," Miller said. "She wasn't old enough."

He replaced the receiver and turned to Brady. "Another possibility we can cross off."

"What now?" Brady demanded.

"I still think there's a lot in this idea of Father Ryan's that Martin wasn't her real name. If that's true, it's just possible she's been listed as a missing person by someone or other. You go and see Chuck Lazer and I'll drop round to the Salvation Army and

see if a chat with Martha Broadribb produces anything."

Brady grinned. "Don't end up beating a drum for
her on Sundays."

But Miller had to force a smile in reply and as he
went down the steps to the car, his face was grim and
serious. At the best of times a good copper was guided
as much by instinct as solid fact and there was something very wrong here, something much more serious than appeared on the surface of things and all
his training, all his experience told him as much.

CHAPTER 4

The small office of the Stone Street Citadel was badly overcrowded, half a dozen young men and women working busily surrounded by green filing cabinets, double-banked to save space.

"I'll see if the Major's in her office," said Miller's escort, a thin, earnest young man in blazer and flannels, and he disappeared in search of Martha Broadribb.

Miller leaned against a filing cabinet and waited, impressed as always at the industry and efficiency so obviously the order of the day. A sheet of writing paper had fallen to the floor and he picked it up and read the printed heading quickly. *Missing Relatives*

Sought in any part of the World: Investigations and Enquiries carried out in Strictest Confidence: Reconciliation Bureau: Advice willingly Given.

The biggest drawback to tracing a missing person from the official point of view was that there was nothing illegal about disappearing. Unless there was a suspicion of foul play, the police could do nothing, which produced the ironical situation that the greatest experts in the field were the Salvation Army, who handled something like ten thousand British and foreign enquiries a year from their Headquarters in Bishopsgate, London, and who were constantly in touch with centres throughout the country such as the Stone Street Citadel.

The young man emerged from the inner office, his arm around the shoulders of a middle-aged woman in a shabby coat who had obviously been weeping. He nodded briefly without speaking and Miller brushed past them and went in.

Major Martha Broadribb was exactly five feet tall, her trim uniformed figure bristling with a vitality that belied her sixty years. Her blue eyes were enormous behind steel-rimmed spectacles and she had the smooth, unused face of an innocent child. And yet this was a woman who had laboured for most of her life in a China Mission, who had spent three terrible years in solitary confinement in a Communist prison camp.

She came forward quickly, a smile of genuine affection on her face. "Nicholas, this *is* nice. Will you have a cup of tea?"

"I wouldn't say no," Miller said. "Who was that who just left?"

"Poor soul. Her husband died a year ago." She took a clean cup and saucer from a cupboard and moved to the tea-tray that stood on her desk. "She married one of her lodgers last month. He persuaded her to sell the house and give him the money she received to buy a business."

"Don't tell me, let me guess," Miller said. "He's cleared off?"

"That's about the size of it."

"She's been to the police?"

"Who told her that as he hadn't committed a criminal offence they were powerless to act." She stirred his tea briskly. "Four lumps and much good may it do you."

"Do you think you'll find him?"

"Certain to," she said, "and he'll face up to his responsibilities and do right by the poor woman after

I've had a chance of talking to him. I'm certain of that."

Another one who thought most people were good at heart. Miller smiled wryly, remembering their first meeting. On his way home one night he had answered an emergency call simply because he happened to be in the vicinity and had arrived at a slum house near the river in time to find a graceless, mindless lout doing his level best to beat his wife to death after knocking Martha Broadribb senseless for trying to stop him, breaking her right arm in the process. And the very next day she had visited him in the Bridewell, plaster-cast and all.

She lit a cigarette, her one vice, and leaned back in her chair. "You look tired, Nicholas."

"I feel tired," he said. "A perpetual state these days, but don't let's go into that." He passed one of the photos across. "Ever seen her?"

Martha examined it with a slight frown. "This is a mortuary photo, isn't it?"

"That's right. I pulled her out of the river this morning."

"Suicide?" There was an expression of real grief on her face. "Poor child. Poor, poor child."

"No ordinary suicide," Miller said. "This girl did

everything she could to destroy her identity before she died."

He sketched in the main facts and she nodded sombrely. "So Father Ryan thinks that Joanna Martin wasn't her real name?"

"He got that impression, which the other two people I've spoken to who knew her confirm. Coming to see you was just a hunch really. I was hoping that somebody might have put out a search for her—that you might recognise her photo."

Martha nodded and held up the medal. "She still hung on to Joanna. Interesting that—they nearly always do hang on to their Christian name. It's as if they're afraid of losing themselves entirely."

She gave him back the medal and made a few notes on her pad. "Let's see what we've got. About nineteen, fair hair, blue eyes. Well spoken, educated, obviously from a superior background and an artist. We'll look under the name of Martin first, just in case, and we'll check the Christian name."

"I didn't know you could do that?"

"As I said, so many of them hang on to their Christian names that it's worth cross-indexing and Joanna isn't very common these days. We'll see what we've got here and I'll also put through a call to

London. Should take about fifteen minutes."

Before he could reply, the 'phone on her desk rang. She took the call and then held out the receiver. "For you—Detective Constable Brady."

Martha went into the outer office and Miller sat on the edge of the desk. "What have you got?"

"Plenty," Brady said. "I've just had a session with a character named Jack Fenner. He's been a registered addict for just over a year now. He makes a living as a dance band drummer."

"I think I've seen him around," Miller said. "Small, fair-haired."

"That's him. He says he had a prescription for heroin and cocaine filled at the all-night chemist's in City Square at midnight on the dot. Joanna Martin stopped him on his way out and offered him a couple of quid for enough pills for a shot. His story is that he felt sorry for her. Said she had the shakes."

"No chance of a mistake?"

"Definitely not." Brady laughed harshly. "In fact this is where it gets interesting. Fenner says he's seen her before."

"Where?"

"At Max Vernon's place, the Flamingo, about six weeks ago. The regular drummer was ill that night and Fenner stood in for him. Apparently it was Vernon's birthday and he threw a big private binge. Fenner remembers the girl because Vernon kept her with him for most of the evening, which Fenner says is highly unusual. Apparently our Max prefers variety."

"Now that *is* interesting," Miller said. "Fenner's certain he's never seen her at any other time?"

"Dead certain—is it important that he should have?"

"Could be. Look at it this way. The girl wasn't a registered addict, we know that, so where did she get the stuff from? If she'd been working the prescription racket outside the all-night chemist's regularly, Fenner would have seen her many times. An addict needs at least one fix a day remember. Usually more."

"Which means that someone must be peddling the stuff?"

"Could be." Behind Miller, the door opened as Martha Broadribb returned and he added hastily, "I've got to go now, Jack. I'll see you back at the office in half an hour."

He turned, eyebrows raised enquiringly, and Martha shook her head. "I'm sorry, Nicholas. Not a thing. There was one Joanna on file, that's all—a West Indian nurse."

Miller sighed and stood up. "Never mind, Martha, it was just a hunch. Thanks for the tea anyway. I'll leave you a copy of the photo just in case."

He dropped it on the desk and as he turned, she placed a hand on his arm, concern on her face. "You're worried about this one, aren't you? There's no need to be. Something will turn up. It always does."

He grinned and kissed her briefly on the forehead. "Don't work too hard, Martha. I'll be seeing you."

The door closed behind him. She stood there staring blankly at it for a moment, then took a deep breath, squaring her shoulders, sat down at her type-writer and started to work.

Brady was sitting on the other side of Grant's desk when Miller looked round the door of the superintendent's office. Grant waved him in at once.

"Jack's been filling me in on your progress so far. You don't seem to be doing too badly. At least you've got a name for her now."

"Which doesn't seem to mean a great deal," Miller said. "I'm afraid Martha Broadribb couldn't help at all."

"Never mind," Grant said. "Something will turn up."

Miller smiled. "The second time I've been told that today. Anything through from C.R.O. on Max Vernon and company yet?"

Grant nodded, his face grim. "And it doesn't make pleasant reading." Brady started to get up and the superintendent waved him down. "You might as well hear this, Jack. I'll be circularising the information anyway."

He put on his reading glasses and picked up the white flimsy that had been delivered from Records ten minutes earlier. "Let's start with his two bully boys and a nice pair they are. Benjamin Carver, 35. Last known profession, salesman. Four previous convictions including five years for robbery with violence; conspiracy to steal; larceny; grievous bodily harm. He's been pulled in for questioning on twenty-three other occasions."

"And Stratton?"

"Even worse. Mad as a March Hare and twisted with it. William, 'Billy' Stratton, 34. Three previous convictions including a five stretch for robbery with violence. Remember the Knavesmire Airport bullion robbery?"

"He was in on that?"

Grant nodded. "The psychiatrists did what they could for him during his last stretch, but it wasn't much. Psychopathic tendencies and too damned handy with a chiv. The next time he stands in the dock it'll be for murder, mark my words."

"And Vernon?"

"Nothing."

"You mean he's clean?" Miller said in astonishment.

"As a whistle." Grant dropped the flimsy on the table. "Six years ago he was invited to help Scotland Yard with their enquiries concerning the Knavesmire Airport bullion robbery. The interview lasted exactly ten minutes, thanks to the best lawyer in London."

"And that's all?"

"All that's official." Grant picked up another flimsy. "Now let's look at what they have to say about him unofficially. Believe me, it'll make your hair stand on end."

"Maxwell Alexander Constable Vernon, 36. Younger son of Sir Henry Vernon, managing director of the Red Funnel shipping line. From Eton he went to Sandhurst and was commissioned in the Guards."

"Only the best, eh?"

Grant nodded. "The rot set in when he was sec-onded for duty with a Malayan infantry regiment during the emergency. Vernon proved so successful at rooting out the Communists in his area that he was awarded the D.S.O. Then they discovered he'd been indulging in an orgy of sadism and torture. No one could afford a public scandal at the time so he was simply persuaded to resign his commission. His fam-ily disowned him."

"He took to crime?"

"That's what it looks like. Organised prostitu-tion—he started with a call-girl racket—illegal clubs, protection, dope peddling—anything that pays, that's our Maxwell. And he's a bright boy—don't make any mistake about that. The Knavesmire Airport heist was only one of half a dozen big jobs he's probably been behind during the past five or six years."

"Why move up here though?" Brady put in. "It doesn't make sense."

"I'm not so sure," Grant said. "Since the middle of last year there's been open warfare in London be-tween the four most powerful gangs, mainly over the protection racket. These things always run to a pat-tern. The villains carve each other up—in this case they're even using shooters—and the police stand by to pick up the pieces when it's all over. Nobody wins that kind of fight and Vernon was clever enough to realise that. As soon as he heard the first rumblings, he sold out to one of his rivals and dropped out of sight."

"To re-appear here?" Brady said.

Grant got to his feet and paced to the window. "I've always thought this might happen one day. That the London mobs would start looking for fresh fields. I'll have to have a word with the old man about it." He shook his head. "I'd love to know what Vernon's been up to since he's been here."

"Maybe Chuck Lazer could give me a few pointers," Miller said.

Grant swung round, his face brightening. "That's a thought. See what you can get out of him."

"I'll do my best," Miller said, "but don't expect too much. To a certain extent Lazer's on the other side of the fence, remember. I'll keep you posted."

He returned to the main C.I.D. room and Brady followed him. "What now?"

"About the girl?" Miller shrugged. "I'm still considering. There are one or two interesting possibilities."

He pulled a packet of cigarettes out of his pocket

and the gold medal and chain fell to the floor. Brady picked it up and examined the inscription again. "At least we know one thing for certain—her Christian name."

Miller paused in the act of lighting his cigarette. "My God, I must be losing my touch."

"What do you mean?" Brady asked.

"I'm remembering something Martha Broadribb told me. How most people who go missing hang on to their Christian name—there's a pretty obvious psychological explanation for that. It's such a common behaviour pattern that they cross-index missing persons under their Christian names as well."

"And where does that get us?" Brady demanded looking puzzled. "She still couldn't help, could she?"

"No, but I'm wondering whether we might have just a little bit more luck at the College of Art," Miller said simply.

"This must be her," Henderson said suddenly, turning from the file and handing Miller a white index card.

He was a small, greying Scot with a pleasant, lined face, obviously fascinated by the present situation, which had turned what would otherwise have been a day of dull routine into a memorable one.

Miller read the details on the card aloud and Brady made notes. "Joanna Maria Craig, address, Rosedene, Grange Avenue, St. Martin's Wood."

Brady pursed his lips in a soundless whistle. "Pretty exclusive. We were certainly on the ball there."

"Apparently she dropped out of the course just over three months ago," Miller said. "It says here see personal file."

"That's what I'm looking for." Henderson had opened another filing cabinet and was flicking rapidly through the green folders it contained. He nodded suddenly, took one out and opened it as he turned

After a while he looked up and nodded. "I remember this case now, mainly because of her father."

"Her father?"

"That's right. A hell of a nice chap. I felt sorry for him at the time. He's managing director of that new firm out on the York Road. Gulf Electronics."

"Why do you say you felt sorry for him?"

"As I recall, she was giving him a hard time. When she first started here everything was fine and then about four months ago she seemed to go to pieces. Cutting lectures, not turning in her work on time, that sort of thing. We called him in to discuss the position." He frowned suddenly. "Now I remember. He brought his other daughter with him. Charming girl. A schoolteacher I believe. It emerged during the interview that he was a widower."

"What happened?"

"He promised to try and straighten the girl out, but I'm afraid he had no luck in that direction. There was a nasty incident about a week later with one of the women lecturers. Harsh words and then the girl slapped her in the face. Naturally she had to go after that."

Miller sat there in silence for a moment, thinking about it, and then got to his feet. He held out his hand. "You've helped us a great deal, Mr. Henderson."

"Anything else I can do don't hesitate to get in touch," Henderson said.

Outside, the pale afternoon sun picked out the vivid colours of the mosaic in the concrete face of the new shopping precinct on the other side of the road and Miller paused at the top of the steps to light a cigarette.

Jack Brady looked up at him, eyebrows raised, and Miller sighed. "And now comes the unpleasant bit."

St. Martin's Wood was on the edge of the city, an exclusive residential area not far from Miller's own home. The houses ran very much to a pattern, turn of the century mansions in grey stone, each one standing in an acre or two of garden. The house they were seeking stood at one end of a quiet cul-de-sac behind a high stone wall. Miller turned the Cooper in through the gates and drove along a wide gravel drive, breaking to a halt at the bottom of a flight of shallow steps which led to the front door.

The bell push was obviously electronic, the sound echoing melodiously inside, and after a while the door was opened by a pleasant-faced young maid in a nylon working overall.

"Yes, sir?" she said to Miller.

"Is Mr. Craig at home by any chance?"

"Colonel Craig," she said in a tone of mild reproof, "is in London at the moment, but we're expecting him home tonight."

"Who is it, Jenny?" a voice called and then a young woman appeared from a door to the right.

"The gentlemen wanted to see the colonel, but I've told them he isn't at home," the maid said.

"All right, Jenny, I'll handle it." She came forward, an open book in one hand. "I'm Harriet Craig. Is there anything I can do?"

She was perhaps twenty-two or -three and nothing like her sister. The black shoulder-length hair framed a face that was too angular for beauty, the mouth so wide that it was almost ugly. And then, for no accountable reason, she smiled and the transformation was so complete that she might have been a different person.

Miller produced his warrant card. "I wonder if we could have a word with you, Miss Craig?"

She looked at the card and frowned. "Is anything wrong?"

"If we could go inside, miss," Brady said gently.

The drawing room into which she led them was beautifully furnished in excellent taste and purple and white hyacinths made a brave splash of colour in a pewter bowl that stood on the grand piano. She turned, a hand on the mantelshelf.

"Won't you sit down?"

Miller shook his head. "I think it might be a good idea if you did."

She stiffened slightly. "You've got bad news for me, is that it?" And then as if by intuition, "Is it my sister? Is it Joanna?"

Miller produced one of the photos from his inside pocket. "Is this her?"

She took the photo from him almost mechanically and her eyes widened in horror. When she spoke, it was in a whisper. "She's dead, isn't she?"

"I'm afraid so," Miller said gently. "She was taken out of the river at dawn today. To the best of our knowledge, she committed suicide."

"Suicide? Oh, my God."

And then she seemed to crack, to break into a thousand fragments and as Miller's arms opened to her, she lurched into them, burying her face against his chest like some small child seeking comfort and strength in a world she could no longer understand.

Jack Palmer lifted the sheet and for a brief moment Harriet Craig looked down on the dead face of her sister. She swayed slightly and Miller's grip tightened on her elbow.

"All right to use your office for ten minutes, Jack?"

"Help yourself."

It was warm in the tiny glass office after the cold outside. Miller sat her in the only chair and perched on the edge of the desk. Jack Brady leaned against the door, notebook and pencil ready.

"I'm afraid I'm going to have to ask you some questions," Miller said.

She nodded, gripping her handbag so tightly that her knuckles gleamed white. "That's all right."

"Were you aware that for the past three months your sister was living at a house in Grosvenor Road under the name of Joanna Martin?"

She shook her head. "No—in fact it doesn't make sense. We understood she was in London. We've had three letters from her and they were all postmarked Chelsea."

"I understand there was some trouble at the College of Art?" Miller said. "That she had to leave? Could you tell me about that?"

"It's rather difficult to explain. Joanna was always a sweet kid. Very talented, but a little naïve, that's why my father thought it would be better to let her attend the local college and live at home instead of going away."

She took a deep shuddering breath and when she continued, her voice was much stronger. "And then, about four months or so ago she seemed to change overnight. It was as if she'd become a different person."

"In what way exactly?"

"Her whole temperament altered. She became violently angry on the slightest excuse. It became almost impossible to handle her. She came home drunk a couple of times and then she started staying out all night. Naturally my father didn't like that, but he's often away on business and in any case, she was hardly a child."

"How old was she?"

"Twenty last month. After a while, there was trouble at the college. She behaved so badly that she was asked to leave."

"What happened then?"

"She had a furious row with my father and ended by packing her bags and leaving. She said she intended to continue her studies at one of the London colleges."

"What about money? Did your father agree to support her?"

"There was no need. She had some of her own. Just over a thousand pounds. A legacy from an old aunt a year or two ago."

"What about boy friends? At the college, for instance?"

"In the two years she was there, she never brought a single one home. As I've said, until that sudden dreadful change in her she was a shy, rather introverted girl, very much bound up in her work."

"Did she ever mention a man named Max Vernon at all?"

Harriet Craig frowned slightly. "Not that I recall. Who is he?"

"Just someone who apparently knew her, but it's of no consequence." Miller hesitated and went on, "Your sister was a drug addict, Miss Craig. Were you aware of that fact?"

His answer was plain in the incredulous horror in her eyes as she looked up at him sharply. Her head moved slightly from side to side, her mouth opened as if to speak, but no sound was uttered.

Miller stood up as she buried her face in her hands and broke into a storm of weeping. He patted her gently on the shoulder and turned to Brady.

"Take her home, Jack. You can use my car."

"What about you?"

"I think I'll have another little chat with Monica Grey and this time I'll have some straight answers. You can catch up with me there."

He went out quickly, fastening the belt of his trenchcoat as he moved along the corridor, and the expression on his face was like the wrath of God.

CHAPTER 5

The door of her room was unlocked and when he opened it gently and went in, she was sitting on the edge of the bed buffing her nails. She glanced up sharply and Miller closed the door.

"Sergeant Miller," she said and then her voice faltered.

Miller produced one of the photos and held it up. "Joanna Maria Craig." He slipped the photo back into his pocket. "Why did you lie to me?"

"I don't know what you mean."

"Joanna Craig was a student at the College of Art for the best part of two years. So were you. And don't try to tell me you never came across her. You were in the same year group. I've just checked."

She stared up at him, her face white, and he took his time over lighting a cigarette. "Another thing. Mrs. Kilroy told me that Joanna had just arrived on the doorstep one day complete with baggage; that there just happened to be a vacancy. Now that isn't true, is it? She knew there was a vacancy because you told her."

She shook her head vigorously. "It isn't true."

"Isn't it? Then try this for size. You work for Max Vernon, don't you?"

And this time he had her. Her eyes widened in horror, and he went on relentlessly, "Joanna was his girl friend—I've got proof. Are you going to try to tell me you didn't know that as well?"

She tried to get to her feet and he flung her back across the bed fiercely. "Come on, damn you! What about the truth for a change?"

She turned her face into the pillow and burst into a flood of tears, her whole body shaking. Miller stood looking down at her, something close to pity in his eyes, and then he moved across the room quickly and went into the small kitchen. He found half a bottle of gin in one of the cupboards, poured a generous measure into a tumbler and went back.

He sat on the edge of the bed and she turned her tear-stained face towards him. "He'll kill me. I know he will."

"No one's going to kill you." Miller held out the glass. "Drink this. You'll feel better."

She struggled up against the pillows. "You don't know what he can be like."

"Max Vernon?"

She nodded and sipped some of her gin. "He's a devil—a walking devil. Cruel, arrogant—anything he wants, he takes."

"And that included Joanna Craig?"

Her eyes widened in amazement. "How did you know that?"

"Just a hunch. But tell me about it—everything that happened."

"All right." She swung her legs to the floor, stood up and paced restlessly about the room as she talked. "You were right about the College of Art. I knew Joanna for nearly two years. Not that we were close friends or anything like that. I liked to live it up. Joanna was more interested in her work."

"What about boy friends?"

"She hardly ever bothered. This may sound crazy to you, but she had something about her. She was sort of untouched by life if you know what I mean."

"I think I do," Miller said.

"Not that there was anything weird about her. Everybody liked her. She was the sweetest person I've ever known, but they treated her with respect, particularly the men. That's something for art students, believe me."

"And yet she changed," Miller said. "So utterly and completely that she might have been a different person. Why?"

"She met Max Vernon."

"I wouldn't have thought he was her type."

"He wasn't—that was the whole trouble." She swallowed the rest of her gin and sat on the edge of the bed. "I answered an advertisement for female croupiers at the Flamingo. As I told you earlier, the money was so good that I dropped out of the college course and started working there. Max was always throwing big parties and he was pretty free and easy about us bringing our friends along."

"You took Joanna to one?"

"That's right. About four months ago. I bumped into her one afternoon quite by chance. There was a party that evening and I asked her to come on impulse. I never expected her to say yes, but she did."

"What happened?"

"Max took a fancy to her. I don't know what it was—maybe it was just her innocence. She was certainly different from every other girl there."

"Did she respond?"

"Anything but and he tried everything, believe me. Then she passed out. I thought that maybe she'd had one gin too many or something. Max took charge. He said she could sleep it off there."

"And you left her?"

"There was nothing I could do." She got to her feet and crossed to the window. "She 'phoned me here next day and asked me to meet her in town. Poor kid, she was in a hell of a state."

"I'm not surprised."

She swung round to face him. "Oh, no, it was worse than that. Much worse. You see someone had given her a fix while she was unconscious."

The bile rose in Miller's throat, threatening to choke him. He got to his feet and walked towards the door, fists clenched and when he turned, she recoiled from the terrible anger on his face.

"Max Vernon?"

"I don't know—I haven't any proof."

Miller crossed the room in three quick strides and

grabbed her savagely by the shoulders. "Was it Max Vernon?"

"Well who the hell else could it have been?" she cried.

For a long moment he held her and when he turned away, she dropped down on to the bed. "She didn't know what had happened to her. All she knew was that her body needed something."

"And only one person was able to supply it," Miller said bitterly. "She wasn't only hooked on heroin and cocaine. She was hooked on Max Vernon."

When Monica Grey continued, her voice was dry and lifeless. "She had a lot of trouble at home and then they asked her to leave at the college. Her whole personality changed. That's how it affects them. I've seen it before."

"So she came to live here with you?"

"Max thought it was a good idea. It's a funny thing, but for a while there I thought he was really gone on her. He had her at the club all the time and if any other man even went near her . . ." She shuddered. "He keeps a couple of heavies around called Carver and Stratton. One night at a party some bloke made a pass at Joanna and they took him out into the alley and half killed him. I heard he lost his right eye. That's the kind they are."

"When did the rot set in?"

She looked up at him quickly. "You don't miss much do you?"

"In my job I can't afford to."

"I don't know what happened, but Max changed towards her just like that about two or three weeks ago."

"She was pregnant, did you know that?"

She shook her head quickly. "No—no I didn't. Maybe that would explain it."

"Did he drop her completely?"

She nodded. "Told her to stay away from the club. She did, too, until last night."

"What happened then?"

"Max was throwing a private party—just a small affair. Mainly personal friends."

"You were there?"

"I'm always there," she said. "All part of the job. Something else he didn't tell me at the interview. Anyway, it must have been about nine o'clock. Things had just started to swing when the door opened and Joanna walked in."

"Just like that?"

"Apparently she still had a key to the private door in the alley. Max was furious. He dragged her into a corner and started telling her where to get off. I couldn't hear what she was saying, but you'd only to see her face to know that she was pleading with him."

"What happened?"

"As I say, I couldn't hear what she said, but he laughed right in her face and said, 'There's always the river, isn't there?' I wasn't the only one who heard that."

There was a long silence and then Miller said calmly, "It would seem she took him at his word." Monica Grey didn't reply and he got to his feet. "Does he know she's dead?"

"Not as far as I'm aware."

"You haven't been in touch with him since I was last here?"

She shook her head and he nodded, moved to the door and opened it. "You do and I'll crucify you."

As he went downstairs, Brady opened the front door. He paused, waiting for Miller to join him. "Any luck?"

"You could say that. How about Harriet Craig?"

"She'll be fine once she gets over the initial shock. She's got a lot about her that one. Where to now?"

"The Flamingo Club," Miller said, "to have a few words with Mr. Maxwell Vernon. I'll explain on the way."

He went down the steps quickly and when he slipped behind the wheel of the Cooper, his hands were shaking.

Max Vernon's office was a showpiece in cream and gold and furnished in perfect taste, the walls lined with expensive military prints, a fire flickering brightly in the Adam grate. He made a handsome figure sitting there at his desk, the last rays of the afternoon sun lighting up the fair hair, picking out the colours of the green velvet smoking jacket, the Guards Brigade scarf at his throat.

There was a knock on the door, it opened and Stratton came in. "I've got those figures you wanted."

Vernon put down his pen and sat back. "Good show, Billy. Just leave 'em on the desk. Anything else?"

"Yes, this copper you were asking about."

"Miller?"

"That's right. You're on a bum steer there. He's anything but bent. It seems his brother owns a chain of television shops. Miller's a sleeping partner, that's where all his gelt comes from."

"But that's illegal," Vernon said. "Coppers aren't encouraged to have business interests on the side."

Stratton nodded. "Apparently they all know about it on the force, but they simply look the other way. It seems Miller's a blue-eyed boy. He's been to University, got a law degree and that sort of thing."

"Has he now?" Vernon said. "Now that *is* interesting."

There was a sudden disturbance in the corridor outside and then the door was thrown open and Miller walked in. Behind him, Jack Brady and Carver glowered at each other, chest to chest. Stratton took one quick, fluid step forward like a ballet dancer, his right hand sliding into his pocket, and Miller raised a finger warningly.

"You do and I'll break your arm."

Vernon sat there, apparently unmoved, a slight smile hooked firmly into place. "Do come in," he said ironically.

"I intend to," Miller told him. "Get rid of these two. We've got business."

"Now look here, you bastard," Carver began and Vernon's voice rang across the room like cold steel.

"I'll call if I need you."

Carver and Stratton obeyed without another murmur and as the door closed behind them, Vernon grinned. "Good discipline—that's what I like to see."

"Once a Guardsman, always a Guardsman, is that it?" Miller said.

"The most exclusive private club in the world." Vernon fitted a cigarette into a green jade holder and gave a mock sigh. "You've been checking up on me, sergeant."

"And how," Miller said. "The Yard was more than interested to hear you'd turned up again."

"Let's get one thing clear," Vernon said. "I run a perfectly legitimate business here and that applies to everything else I own. If you've anything else to say, I suggest you discuss it with my lawyers."

He reached for the telephone and Miller said calmly, "We pulled Joanna Craig out of the river this morning, Vernon."

For a brief moment only Vernon's hand tightened

on the 'phone and then an expression of shock appeared on his face.

"Joanna—in the river? But this doesn't make sense. You're quite sure it is her?"

"Why shouldn't we be?"

"The fact is, I understood she'd been living under an assumed name. Nothing sinister—just to stop her family from running her down. She'd had trouble at home." He shook his head. "This is terrible—terrible."

It was all there, beautifully detailed by a steeltrap mind which had assessed the situation in a matter of seconds and had come up with the only possible counter with the speed of a computer.

"When did you first meet her?"

The answer came without the slightest hesitation. "About four months ago. Someone brought her along to one of my parties. I discovered she was a very talented artist. I wanted some murals for the club and she agreed to accept the commission. It was as simple as that."

"And that was all—just a business arrangement?"

"The murals are on the wall of the main casino, you can see them for yourself," Vernon said.

"Anything else that was between us is no damned business of yours. She wasn't a child. She had a good body and she liked the pleasures of the flesh as much as the rest of us."

"So you did have an affair with her?"

"If you mean by that did she ever sleep with me, the answer is yes. If you're really interested, so do lots of other women, though I can't see what in the hell it has to do with you."

"Did you know she was a junkie—that she was mainlining on heroin?"

"Good heavens, no."

"Not good enough. You didn't even bother to look surprised." Miller shook his head. "You're a liar."

Something glowed deep in Vernon's eyes. "Am I?"

Miller gripped the edge of the desk to keep his hands from shaking. "I know this girl, Vernon. The first time I clapped eyes on her, she was floating off the central quay two feet under the surface and yet I know more about her now than I do about my own sister. She was a sweet, shy girl, a little bit introverted, interested only in her work. To use an old-fashioned word for these times, she was a lady—a term that wouldn't mean a damned thing to you in spite of Eton, Sandhurst and the Guards."

"Is that a fact now," Vernon said softly.

"You're from under a stone, Vernon, did you know that?" Miller said. "Now let me tell you what really happened between you and Joanna Craig. She was brought to one of your parties by an old student friend and she must have looked as fresh as the flowers in spring compared to the usual rubbish you keep around. You wanted her, but she didn't want you and that wasn't good enough for the great Maxwell Vernon because what he wants he takes. You got her boozed up and gave her a fix and from then on she was hooked because she had to have one every day of the week and that meant coming to you—accepting your terms. That's the terrible thing about addiction to heroin. There's no degradation to which the victim won't stoop to get the stuff and you must have been just about as low as she could get."

Vernon's face was white, the eyes burning. "Have you quite finished?"

"I'll let you know when I have. When you'd had enough, you threw her out and then last night she forced her way into your party to beg you to help her because she was going to have a baby. You laughed in her face, Vernon. You told her there was always the river and she took you at your word." Miller straightened up and took a deep breath. "I'm going to get you for that."

"Are you now?" Vernon said calmly. "Well let me tell you something, Mr. Bloody Miller. I knew a girl called Joanna Craig just like I know a hell of a lot of other girls. She painted some murals in the main casino downstairs. You or anyone else can see them whenever you like. Anything else is pure phantasy. You try bringing it out in an open court and I'll knock you down so hard you'll never get up again. Now I'm giving you one minute to get out of here or I'm calling my lawyer and you know what that means."

"Perfectly," Miller said. "It means you're frightened to death." He smiled coldly. "See you in court, Vernon."

He turned and nodded to Brady who opened the door and they went out. For a while Vernon sat there staring into space and then he lifted the 'phone and pushed a button.

"Is that you, Ben?" he said. "Send Stratton up right away. I've got a little job for him."

. . .

Monica Grey came out of the bathroom listlessly. She'd hoped a good hot tub would make her feel better. Instead, she felt depressed, drained of all energy. How she was going to get through the long night at the Flamingo, she didn't know.

The knock, when it came, was so faint that at first she thought she'd imagined it. She hesitated, fastening the belt of her robe quickly, and it sounded again.

When she opened the door, she had a vague impression of someone standing there, of an arm sweeping up and then liquid splashed across her face. She staggered back, a scream rising in her throat, her hands covering her eyes as they began to burn. She was aware of the door closing and then a hand slammed against her shoulder, spinning her round so that she fell across the bed.

Someone laughed coldly and fingers fastened in her hair, jerking her head back painfully. "Come on now, dearie, open up for Uncle Billy."

She opened her eyes, aware that the smarting had somehow eased, and looked into Billy Stratton's white, bloodless face. Only his lips had any colour and he smiled showing a row of sharp, even teeth.

"Water, dearie, mixed with a little disinfectant to make your eyes sting. Just imagine what it could have been—vitriol, for instance." He chuckled mirth-lessly. "You'd have been blind now."

She was absolutely terrified and lay there staring up at him in horror as he patted her on the cheek. "You've been a naughty girl, haven't you? You've been talking to the wrong people. Mr. Vernon doesn't like that—he doesn't like that at all. Now get your clothes on. You're coming with me."

It was almost dusk when Miller turned the Cooper in through the gates of the house in Grange Avenue and braked to a halt at the bottom of the steps leading up to the front door. It had been a long day and he was so tired that he sat at the wheel for a moment before getting out.

When he rang the bell, the door was opened by Jenny, the young maid, and her eyes were red and swollen from weeping. "Sergeant Miller," she said. "You'd better come in."

"There was a message for me at Headquarters," Miller said. "Apparently Colonel Craig called at the Mortuary to view his daughter's body. I understand he'd like to see me."

"The Colonel and Miss Harriet are out walking

in the garden," Jenny said. "I'll get him for you."

"That's all right," Miller told her. "I'll find him for myself."

It was cold in the garden and rooks cawed uneasily in the bare branches of the beech trees as he crossed the lawn already damp with the evening dew. Somewhere there was a low murmur of voices above the rattle of a small stream over stones and then a familiar voice called to him on the quiet air. "Over here, Sergeant Miller."

Harriet Craig leaned against the rail of a tiny rustic bridge. The man who stood with her was perhaps a shade under six feet in height with iron grey hair cut close to his skull.

The eyes were very calm above high cheekbones. For a moment they considered Miller and then he held out his hand. "It was good of you to come so quickly."

There was an extraordinary impression of vitality about him, of controlled force that Miller found strangely disturbing. He must have been at least forty-eight or -nine and yet he carried himself with the easy confidence of a man half his age.

"Your message said that you'd like to talk things

over with me," Miller said. "I'll be happy to help in any way I can."

"I've seen your Superintendent Grant," Colonel Craig said. "He gave me as comprehensive a report as he could, but felt that the full details would be better coming from you." He hesitated and then went on, "I believe Harriet gave you some indication of the trouble we were having with Joanna."

"That's right."

"I've been given to understand that she'd become addicted to the drug heroin."

"Which explains what otherwise would have been her completely inexplicable change in character," Miller told him. "You must understand that heroin produces a feeling of well-being and buoyancy, but in between fixes an addict is sick, unwell and has only one thought in mind—to get another fix. They become paranoid, irritable, subject to extremes of emotion."

"And that's what happened to Joanna?"

"The girl who gave you all that trouble wasn't your daughter, colonel," Miller said gently. "She only looked like her."

For a long, long moment there was silence and

then Colonel Craig said, "Thank you for that, sergeant. And now, if you don't mind, I'd like you to tell me everything—everything there is to know about this whole sorry affair."

It didn't take long, that was the strange thing, and when he had finished, Harriet Craig leaned against the rail crying quietly, her father's arm about her shoulders.

"This man Vernon," Craig said. "He'll be called as a witness at the inquest?"

"That's right."

"Is there any possibility of a criminal charge being preferred against him?"

Miller sighed heavily and shook his head. "I might as well be honest with you. I don't hold out much hope."

"But he murdered Joanna," Harriet Craig cried passionately. "Murdered her as surely as if he'd used a gun or a knife."

"I know that," Miller said. "Morally he's as guilty as any man could be, but the facts are all that matters and this is how it will look in court. Your sister committed suicide. She was pregnant and she was also a drug addict. One witness, Monica Grey, has indicated that someone gave your daughter an injection of heroin at a party at Max Vernon's after she'd passed out, but even she can't swear definitely that it was Vernon. She wouldn't last five minutes on the stand with the kind of counsel he'd bring in. Another thing, this isn't a criminal matter at the moment. All she's done is give me a general verbal statement that she might change completely once she's on the stand."

"But Vernon was responsible," Harriet said. "He was responsible for everything. You believe that yourself."

"Proving it is something else again."

There was another long silence and then Craig said, "There's just one thing I don't understand. Joanna did everything she could to conceal her identity before she killed herself. Why would she do that?"

"Do you really want me to answer that, colonel?"

"More than anything else in the world."

"All right. I'd say she did it for you."

The expression on Craig's face didn't alter. "Please go on."

"In those final moments, I think she must have been thinking more clearly than she had for a long time. She'd let you down enough. She didn't want to shame you any more. I think she wanted the river to swallow her up as if she'd never been."

When Craig replied, only the slightest of tremor disturbed the even tenor of his voice. "Thank you, sergeant. Somehow I thought it might be something like that."

CHAPTER 6

When Brady opened the door of the Coroner's Court and peered inside, proceedings had already started. In spite of the fact that there were no more than half a dozen members of the public present, the court seemed overcrowded with the jury taking up almost one side of the room and the coroner high above them on the bench, the court officers below.

Miller was just leaving the stand. He noticed Brady at once and they went outside quietly and closed the door.

"Sorry I'm late," Brady said. "I had a remand. How's it going?"

"I've just done my little act. Craig's down front

with Harriet. Vernon's got Henry Baxter with him."

"That old shark?" Brady whistled. "He'll charge him plenty."

"Any word from Grant?"

Brady nodded. "Not good I'm afraid. He's just heard from the office of the Director of Public Prosecutions. They've considered the matter and as far as they're concerned, there isn't even the beginnings of a case against Vernon."

"Never mind. It was worth a try and there's still the hearing. You can never be sure what's going to happen at a coroner's inquest."

They went back inside and sat down in time to hear Monica Grey take the oath.

"You are Monica Alice Grey and you reside at 15, Argyle Road?"

"That's right."

"When did you first meet the deceased?"

"About two years ago. We were both students at the College of Art."

"We have heard from Detective Sergeant Miller that she came to reside at the same address as yourself under the name of Joanna Martin. Why was that?"

"She was having trouble at home. She decided to

leave, but she didn't want her father to know where she was living."

Miller leaned forward slightly, intent on the proceedings. In his own case he had been compelled to stick strictly to the facts and what Monica Grey said from now on was going to be of crucial importance.

"You were on close terms with the deceased?"

"We were good friends—yes."

"She confided in you—discussed her troubles. For example, were you aware that she was a drug addict?"

"I was, but only found out by accident. I happened to go into her room one day and found her giving herself a fix."

The coroner glanced over the top of his spectacles sharply. "I beg your pardon?"

"An injection of heroin."

"And did she tell you what had started her on the habit?"

"Yes, she said she'd passed out after having too much to drink at some party or other. Someone had given her an injection while she was unconscious."

"Why would anyone do that?"

"I don't know. For a giggle, maybe."

"Indeed." The coroner examined the papers in front of him, his face impassive. "Did she ever suggest to you that the party in question was at a gaming club called the Flamingo owned by Mr. Maxwell Vernon?"

"Definitely not."

The coroner looked at her steadily for a moment and then nodded. "You were aware that she was pregnant?"

"Yes, she told me a couple of weeks ago."

"In what circumstances?"

"She was very upset. She asked me if I knew anyone who could help her."

"To get rid of the child?"

"That's right."

The coroner made another note. "One final question. As regards the state of mind of the deceased. Would you say she was a balanced individual?"

Monica Grey shook her head. "Not during the time she lived with me. She sometimes had terrible bouts of depression, but I think that was the drugs."

"Thank you, that will be all."

The fat, well-dressed man who was sitting at the front beside Vernon half rose and the coroner stayed Monica Grey with his hand. "Yes, Mr. Baxter."

"I appear on behalf of Mr. Maxwell Vernon, called as a witness in this matter. Certain rumours seem to be circulating which connect my client and the deceased. I think we might be able to clarify the situation if I could put a question or two to Miss Grey."

"By all means."

"I shan't keep you long, Miss Grey," Baxter said. "I'd like to return to this question of the deceased's pregnancy. Did she ever tell you who the father was?"

"I asked her, but she wouldn't disclose his name."

"It has been alleged in certain quarters that my client was responsible."

"He couldn't have been."

"You seem very positive. Might I ask why?"

Monica Grey hesitated, glanced across at Vernon and said with obvious reluctance, "To tell you the truth, I knew Joanna had been out with Mr. Vernon a few times and I thought it might be him. When I put it to her she said definitely not. That it was someone else entirely."

"A last question, Miss Grey. I understand you were present at a private party given by Mr. Vernon at his flat at the Flamingo Club on the night the deceased died."

"That's right."

"Please tell us what happened."

"It was about nine o'clock. The party had just got started when Joanna walked in. She was in a bit of a state so Mr. Vernon took her into the corner to calm her down."

"Could you hear their conversation?"

"Not really. She was obviously very upset and Mr. Vernon seemed to be trying to take her out of herself. After a while she just turned and walked out."

"What did Mr. Vernon do?"

"He took me on one side and said he hadn't liked the way she was talking. He asked me to keep an eye on her, to let him know if there was anything he could do."

"Thank you, Miss Grey."

Monica Grey returned to her seat as Baxter sat down and Vernon was called. He made an impressive figure in the dock, erect and manly in a well-cut suit, the Guards tie standing out against a snow white shirt. His occupation was given as company director, which made the impression on the jury that Miller had expected.

"Mr. Vernon, how long had you known the deceased?"

"About four months," Vernon said. "Miss Monica Grey, an employee of mine, brought her to a party at my place one night. I understood they'd been students together."

"And you became close friends?"

"I think it would be fair to say that." Vernon shrugged. "As an artist, she had real talent and I admired her work. I commissioned her to paint a series of murals at my club."

"I see." The coroner's voice was dry, remote. "Was the relationship ever anything more than a business one?"

"I took her to dinner now and then or to the theatre. We got on very well together. I liked her immensely."

"And on occasion you were intimate with her?"

Vernon managed to inject just the right amount of outrage into his voice when he replied. "The girl's dead, damn you! Can't she be left in peace!"

There was a flurry of movement amongst the jury, an outburst of whispering. One man even nodded approvingly and the coroner had to call for silence.

He removed his spectacles and leaned back in his chair.

"Mr. Vernon, I can respect your feelings in this

matter, but I must insist on a reply—and you are still under oath, sir."

Vernon's shoulders sagged. "Yes, we were intimate." He drew himself up suddenly and glared fiercely at the coroner. "And why not? She wasn't a child. It was our own affair."

The coroner replaced his spectacles and examined the papers before him again. "Were you aware that she had become a drug addict?"

"Certainly not. Do you think I could have stood by and done nothing if I'd known?"

"We've already heard that on the night she died, she appeared at a private party you were giving at your club."

"That's right."

"What happened on that occasion?"

"There really isn't much to tell. She was depressed and unhappy. She told me that she'd lost the urge to paint, that life didn't seem worth living any longer. I realise, in retrospect, that it was the drugs which had reduced her to that state. I advised her to go home. She'd told me previously that she and her father hadn't been seeing eye to eye, but it seemed to me that didn't matter any longer. That home was the best place for her."

"How did she react to that advice?"

"She didn't, I'm afraid. I went to get her a drink. When I returned, she'd gone."

"Thank you, Mr. Vernon. You may stand down."

As Vernon went back to his seat, Baxter rose again. "If I might insert a word at this time on my client's behalf?"

The coroner nodded and Baxter continued, "Certain allegations do seem to have been made in connection with this unfortunate young woman's death, allegations which would suggest that my client was in some way responsible. I would suggest his complete honesty in answering the question put to him, and his bearing on the stand, added to the statement of Miss Monica Grey, an independent witness, make nonsense of these allegations, which are completely without foundation. My client is Managing Director of a company which controls several important enterprises. I might also add, although he has attempted to dissuade me from so doing, that he was at one time a regular officer in the Brigade of Guards and in 1951 was awarded the Distinguished Service Order for gallantry and outstanding leadership during the Malayan Emergency."

Vernon looked suitably embarrassed as Baxter sat

down. "Thank you, Mr. Baxter," the coroner said. "Call Colonel Craig, please."

All eyes turned on Craig as he got to his feet and moved to the stand. He stood there, hands resting lightly on the rail, the eternal soldier in spite of his dark suit and tie.

"You are Colonel Duncan Stuart Craig and you reside at Rosedene, Grange Avenue, St. Martin's Wood?"

"That is correct."

"Did you see the body of a woman at the City Mortuary on Tuesday of this week?"

"I did."

"Who was she?"

"My daughter—Joanna Maria Craig."

"I will issue you with a burial order." There was a pause as the coroner made a note and he continued, "I know this must be most distressing for you, Colonel Craig, so I shan't keep you long. Until four months ago or thereabouts, your daughter was a perfectly normal young woman for her age in every way?"

"That is so. The change, when it came, was inexplicable to us. Temper tantrums, extremely emotional behaviour, that sort of thing. She became a completely different person. I realise now that her general deterioration was a direct consequence of her addiction to heroin."

"From the time your daughter left home until her death did she ever communicate with you?"

"There were three letters, all postmarked Chelsea. They are before the court."

The coroner nodded. "I have read them. They would seem to imply that she was residing in London and studying at a College of Art there. Presumably some acquaintance posted them for her." He hesitated and then went on, "Colonel Craig, you have heard the evidence before the court. Have you anything to add?"

Miller felt Brady stir beside him and held his breath, waiting for Craig's answer. "I have nothing to add, sir. The evidence in this matter seems clear enough."

"And you can make of that what you like," Brady whispered to Miller.

And then, with a rush, it was all over. The jury didn't even bother to retire and the foreman, a small, greying bank clerk, rose self-consciously. "We find that the deceased took her own life while the balance of her mind was disturbed."

"And that is the verdict of you all." The foreman nodded and sat down. "Let it so be entered."

There was a sudden hush as people sat up expectantly, waiting for the coroner's closing words. "It is not within my province to make moral judgements. It is sufficient for me to say that on the evidence presented I must agree completely with the verdict of the jury. There is one disturbing feature of this case and it is this. Joanna Craig was not a registered drug addict and yet somehow or other she managed to obtain a daily supply. I trust that the representatives of the police present in court will see that this aspect of the affair is most thoroughly investigated."

"The court will rise for Her Majesty's Coroner."

There was a general move towards the exit and Brady turned towards Miller, his face grim. "And that's that. The swine's got away with it."

"What else did you expect?" Miller said.

Colonel Craig and Harriet were still sitting down at the front and Vernon and Baxter had to pass them. For a moment, Vernon hesitated as if about to speak and then obviously thought better of it. He nodded to Miller and Brady as he passed them, face grave, and went out.

"I wonder what Craig would have done if the

bastard had tried to speak to him?" Brady said.

Craig came towards them, Harriet hanging on to his arm. He smiled tightly. "Have you gentlemen time for a drink?"

Brady shook his head reluctantly. "Not me, I'm afraid. I'm in court again in ten minutes." He nodded to Miller. "I'll catch up with you later."

For the moment, they had the court to themselves and Harriet Craig said bitterly, "Justice—is that what they call it?"

"I'm sorry," Miller said. "More sorry than I can say. We tried the Director of Public Prosecutions but he told us we hadn't got even the shadow of a case. I was hoping something might come out at the hearing. As you probably noticed, things are pretty informal in a coroner's court. No one get's worked up over procedure and so on which usually means that things have a chance to break through to the surface."

"But not in this case, it would appear."

Craig put an arm around her shoulders and gave her a quick squeeze. "Let's have that drink, shall we? Do us all good."

They sat in the saloon bar of the George across the square and Craig ordered brandy all round and offered Miller a cigarette while they waited. Behind them, the bar was lined with solicitors and their clerks and councils in wig and gown, most of them snatching a beer and a sandwhich between cases and talking shop.

Harriet leaned across and covered one of Miller's hands with her own. "I'm sorry I sounded off back there in court. I wasn't getting at you. You believe that, don't you?"

"That's all right."

"You know Vernon's a very clever man," Craig said. "He handled himself superbly. Made an excellent impression on the jury."

"And the girl helped, don't forget that," Miller said.

"Yes, she lied, didn't she?"

"Too true she did, probably under extreme coercion." Miller hesitated and then went on. "It wasn't her fault, you know. She's just as much a victim of circumstances as Joanna was. Actually, she's quite a nice girl."

Craig swirled the brandy around in his glass and drank some. "You know I've been finding out a few things about our Mr. Vernon. He's quite a character."

"Is that so?" Miller said carefully.

"Come off it, sergeant, you know what I mean." Craig swallowed the rest of his brandy and waved to the waiter for another. "You've heard of Pedlar Palmer, I suppose?"

"Detective Superintendent Palmer of the Special Branch at Scotland Yard?"

"That's right. We did some soldiering together in the Middle East back in '43. I gave him a ring yesterday, just to ask him what he could tell me about Vernon. He owes me a favour or two. That's in confidence, mind you."

"Naturally."

"Quite a boy, Max Vernon. Do you think he's getting up to the same sort of capers in these parts as he did in London?"

"Leopards don't change their spots."

"That's what I thought." Craig nodded, a slight, abstracted smile on his face. "What is it they say about justice, sergeant? It must not only be done, it must be seen to be done? But what happens when society falls down on the job? What happens when the law isn't adequate? Wouldn't you say the individual was entitled to take matters into his own hands?"

"I know one thing," Miller said. "It wouldn't be the law he was taking."

"You've got a good point there." Craig glanced at his watch. "Good heavens, is that the time? I must go. Can you get a taxi, Harriet?"

Miller cut in quickly before she could reply. "I'll see she gets home all right. I have my own car."

"Thanks a lot. I'll see you later then, my dear." He squeezed Harriet's shoulder briefly and was gone.

"Another drink, Miss Craig?"

"No, I don't think so. I'd like to go if you don't mind. I'm feeling rather tired. These past few days have been something of a strain."

The Mini-Cooper was in for servicing and he was using his brother's E-type Jaguar that day. She was suitably impressed. "I didn't know police pay had improved quite this much."

"It hasn't," he said as he handed her in and closed the door. "This belongs to my brother. He has more money than he knows what to do with and he worries about me."

He took the car out into the main traffic stream expertly. "You're a teacher, aren't you?"

She nodded. "That's right. Dock Street Secondary Modern. I took the day off."

"A pretty rough neighbourhood."

"Good experience. They're pulling the school

down soon. There'll be a new Comprehensive opening about half a mile away."

They drove in silence for a while and then he said,
"You don't think your father will try to do anything
silly, do you?"

She frowned. "What on earth do you mean?"

"I wasn't too happy about that conversation we
had back at the pub. All that stuff about taking the
law into one's own hands when society falls down
on the job."

"It's worth a thought, isn't it?"

Miller shook his head. "Not if he wants to stay
alive. Max Vernon's a powerful, ruthless criminal
without the slightest scruples about who he hurts or
how he does it. He'd crush your father like an ant
under his foot."

She turned on him, her mouth slack with amazement. "Crush Duncan Craig—that worm?" She
laughed wildly. "Don't you know who my father is?
If he's made the decision I think he has, then Maxwell
Vernon is a dead man walking."

CHAPTER 7

When Monica Grey opened her door and found Duncan Craig standing there, she tried to close it quickly, but he was inside before she could stop him.

She backed away, her throat going dry, and he shook his head slowly. "I'm not going to hurt you, I'm not going to harm you in any way. Just sit down like a good girl and listen to me."

Suddenly she was no longer afraid. In fact for some strange reason she felt like crying and she did as she was told and slumped down on the bed.

"You lied at the inquest, didn't you?"

"I had to. God knows what would have happened to me if I hadn't done as I was told."

"Then your original statement to Sergeant Miller was true? It was Max Vernon who first gave my daughter heroin?"

"It had to be him," she said. "It couldn't have been anyone else."

"And Vernon who continued to supply her."

She nodded. "One of his little sidelines."

"You know a great deal about him, don't you?"

"Plenty," she said, "but you needn't think I'm going to sing out in open court for you or anyone else."

"You won't have to. Have you got a passport?"

She nodded. "Somewhere around the place. Why?"

He took a large buff envelope from his inside breast pocket. "You'll find traveller's cheques in here for one thousand pounds plus a ticket on the four-thirty flight to London Airport."

"And just how long do you think it would take Max Vernon to catch up with me?"

"At least a couple of days. Long enough for you to complete any formalities, have any necessary inoculations and so on. You'll find another plane ticket in the envelope—a first-class single to Sydney. You could be on your way by Wednesday."

"You mean Sydney, Australia?"

"That's right. You'll also find a letter to a business friend of mine out there. He'll fix you up with a job and help you get started. You'll be all right. He owes me a favour."

Her eyes were shining and the lines had been wiped clean from her forehead. Colonel Craig laid the envelope down on the bed beside her.

"In return I want you to tell me everything there is to know about Max Vernon."

She didn't hesitate. "It's a deal. You talk and I'll pack."

"They tell me he was the brains behind one or two big jobs in the London area. The Knavesmire Airport bullion robbery for instance. Has he pulled anything like that up here?"

"Not as far as I know, but I think there's something in the wind. There's been some funny customers in and out of the place lately."

"What about the Flamingo? Is the game honest?"

"It has to be." She pulled a suitcase down from the top of the wardrobe. "It caters for the most exclusive clientele in town."

"You wouldn't have a key to the place by any chance?"

"Sure—to the back door." She opened her handbag, produced a Yale key and threw it across. "My pleasure."

"What other little enterprises does Vernon operate?"

"There's the betting shops."

"I'm looking for something rather more illegal."

"That's easy. He runs a cut liquor still up the York Road. Gibson's Furniture Factory it says outside, but it's a front. Supplies clubs all over the north."

"Where does the liquor come from in the first place?"

"Your guess is as good as mine. Some from long distance lorries that took the wrong turning. Some they make on the premises. He's got money tied up in that place."

"But more still in the Flamingo?"

She fastened the lid on one suitcase and took down another. "Better than a hundred thousand. Without the Flamingo he's nothing. He had to take what he could get when he sold up in London. They say he dropped a bundle."

"And what about the betting shops?"

"He operates them on a day-to-day basis using the cash from the previous night's take at the

Flamingo. He still hasn't got on his feet up here yet."

"So everything revolves around the Flamingo."

"I suppose you could say that." She frowned suddenly. "What are you getting at?"

"Never you mind, you've got other things to think about now." He glanced at his watch. "We'll have to get moving. We've got exactly half an hour to get you to the airport."

The Bull & Bell Yard was not far from the market, a dirty and sunless cobbled alley named after the public house which had stood there for more than two hundred years. Beside the entrance to the snug stood several overflowing dustbins and cardboard boxes and packing cases were thrown together in an untidy heap.

It was raining slightly and an old man squatted against the wall, a bottle of beer in one hand, a sandwich in the other. He wore an ancient army greatcoat and his hair and beard were long and matted.

The door opened and a barman appeared in the entrance, a bucket in one hand. He was a large, hefty young man in a white apron with long dark sideburns and a cold, rather dangerous face. He emptied the bucket of slops across the cobbles and looked down at the old man in disgust.

"You still here, Sailor? Christ Jesus, I don't know how you can stand it."

"Go on, Harry," the old man said hoarsely. "Ain't doing any 'arm, am I?"

The barman went back inside and Sailor raised the bottle of beer to his lips. He lowered it slowly, his mouth gaping in amazement. The man who stood facing him had the most extraordinary eyes the Sailor had ever seen, quite dark and completely expressionless. He wore a three-quarter length British warm, a bowler hat and carried a tightly rolled umbrella.

His hand disappeared into a pocket and came out holding a pound note. "Do you know Mr. Vernon?" he said. "Mr. Max Vernon?" Sailor nodded. "Is he inside?"

"In the snug, governor."

The man in the bowler hat dropped the pound note into his lap. "I'm very much obliged to you," he said and went inside.

Sailor waited for no more than a moment and then he scrambled to his feet, pushed open the door an inch or two and peered in.

The Bull & Bell did ninety-five per cent of its trade in the evenings, which was why Max Vernon preferred to patronise it in the afternoon. For one thing it meant that he could have the snug to himself, which was handy for business of a certain kind.

He sat on a stool at the bar finishing a roast beef sandwich, a pint of bitter at his elbow, and Carver and Stratton lounged on the window seat chatting idly.

It was Carver who first noticed Craig standing in the doorway. "Christ Almighty," he said and then there was a long silence.

Craig moved into the snug and paused against the bar three or four feet away from Vernon. "There you are, Vernon. You know you're a damned difficult fellow to run down. I've been looking everywhere for you."

"I'm in the telephone book, colonel," Vernon said calmly.

"Ah, but that wouldn't have suited my purpose at all, I'm afraid," Craig said. "What I was hoping for was a private chat—just the two of us."

He glanced at Carver and Stratton and Vernon shrugged. "There's nothing you can say to me that these two can't hear."

"Suit yourself." Craig took a cigarette from a pigskin case and lit it carefully. "I expect you'll be wondering why Monica Grey didn't turn up for work last night. She gave me a message for you."

"Did she now?"

"I'm afraid you'll have to manage without her in future." Craig blew smoke up towards the ceiling in a long streamer. "Actually I had a very informative chat with her after which I put her on a plane with a first-class ticket to somewhere so far away that she can forget she ever knew a man called Max Vernon."

"What is this?" Vernon said. "A declaration of war?"

"To the knife," Craig said pleasantly. "First of all I'm going to destroy the things that are important to you, Vernon. After that, and only when I'm ready, I'm going to destroy you."

Stratton took a sudden step forward and Vernon raised his hand quickly. "Stay where you are!" He looked Craig up and down and shook his head slowly. "It's been tried, colonel. It's been tried by the best in the business and they all ended up flat on their faces."

"But you did have to get out of London in rather a hurry."

"So what—I'll be up there on top again. I'm on my way now. I'll run this town before I'm finished."

"The great Max Vernon," Craig said. "He always gets what he wants."

"That's it."

"Including my daughter."

"Including your daughter. She saw things my way by the time I was through with her."

For the first time, Craig's iron composure cracked and his hand tightened around the handle of his umbrella. He half raised it as if to strike, but quickly regained control.

"Thank you for saying that, Vernon. You've made it a lot easier for me."

Vernon's easy smile vanished in an instant. "You know something, you remind me of my old colonel. I couldn't stand him either. Harry!" he called. "Get in here!"

Harry came in from the other bar drying a pewter tankard. "Yes, Mr. Vernon?"

Vernon nodded towards Craig and picked up his newspaper. "Get rid of him."

"Certainly, Mr. Vernon." Harry lifted the bar flap

and moved out. "Right, on your way, mate."

"I'll go when I'm ready," Craig said pleasantly.

Harry's right hand fastened on Craig's collar and they went through the door with a rush to a chorus of laughter from Stratton and Carver. As the door to the alley burst open, Sailor ducked behind a packing case and waited.

Harry was grinning widely, an arm around Craig's throat. "We don't like fancy sods like you coming around here annoying the customers." He didn't get the chance to say anything else. Craig's right elbow swung back sharply connecting just beneath the ribs and, as Harry swung back gasping, he pivoted on one foot.

"You should never let anyone get that close. They haven't been teaching you properly."

Harry gave a cry of rage and sprang forward, his right fist swinging in a tremendous punch. Craig grabbed for the wrist with both hands and twisted it round and up so that he held him in a Japanese shoulder lock. Harry cried out in agony and still keeping that terrible hold in position, Craig ran him head-first into the stack of packing cases. As he bent down to retrieve his umbrella, Vernon appeared in the doorway, Carver and Stratton crowding behind him.

Craig nodded briefly. "I'll be in touch, Vernon," he said and walked briskly away.

It was perhaps ten minutes later that the 'phone rang on Nick Miller's desk in the main C.I.D. room. He picked up the receiver at once and a familiar voice roughened by years of drink and disease sounded in his ear.

"That you, Sergeant Miller? This is Sailor—Sailor Hagen. I'm ringing from a call box in City Square. I've got something good for you. What's it worth?"

"Depends what it's about," Miller said.

"The bloke who took over Harry Faulkner's place, the Flamingo. Max Vernon."

Miller was already on his feet. "I'll meet you by the fountain in five minutes," he said and hung up.

When Miller was shown in, Vernon was in the main casino looking over arrangements for the evening opening. "You're getting to be a permanent fixture around here," he said.

"You can cut out the funny stuff," Miller told him. "What happened at the Bull & Bell?"

"I haven't the slightest idea what you're talking about."

"Duncan Craig visited you there no more than an hour ago. As I understand it, he threatened to kill you."

Vernon leaned against the edge of the roulette table and laughed gently. "Someone's been pulling your leg, old man."

"This is serious, Vernon," Miller said. "I don't give a damn what happens to you, but I do care what happens to Duncan Craig."

Vernon shrugged. "As far as I'm concerned the whole thing's over and done with." He glanced at his watch. "They're burying his daughter at St. Gemma's Church at four o'clock. I sent a wreath. Could I do more than that?"

"You did what?" Miller said incredulously.

Vernon smiled blandly. "One does have to do the right thing on these occasions."

When Miller's hands came out of their pockets, they were both tightly clenched. For a long, long moment he stood there fighting the impulse to knock Vernon's teeth down his throat and then he swung on his heel and walked rapidly towards the exit. Behind him, Vernon started to laugh gently.

It was raining quite hard when Miller drove up to St. Gemma's. He parked the Cooper in the main

road and went in through the side gate and along a
narrow path lined with poplars leading to the cemetery.

He could hear Father Ryan's voice as he went forward and then he saw them. There were no more
than half a dozen people grouped around the open
grave and the old priest's voice sounded brave and
strong as the rain fell on his bare head.

Miller moved off the path and stood behind a large
marble tomb and after a while, Father Ryan finished
and the group broke up. Harriet Craig was crying
steadily and moved away in company with Jenny, the
young maid, and Father Ryan followed them. Craig
was left standing on his own beside the grave and
Miller went forward slowly.

"It wouldn't work," he said softly. "It wouldn't
bring Joanna back."

Craig turned to face him. "What are you, a mind
reader or something?"

"I know what happened at the Bull & Bell this afternoon."

"I haven't the slightest idea what you're talking
about."

"That's what Vernon said when I called on him.
But someone dislocated Harry Parson's shoulder

and broke his nose. Who the hell was that? Mr. Nobody?"

Craig looked down into the open grave. "She was a nice kid, sergeant. A lot of dreams gone up in smoke there."

"I'm sorry about the wreath," Miller said.

Craig turned, frowning. "What wreath?"

"The wreath Vernon sent. God knows where he gets his gall from."

"I'm happy to say you've been misinformed," Duncan Craig said. "We've certainly received no wreath from Max Vernon." As the rain increased into a solid downpour he turned up his collar. "You must excuse me now, but Harriet's taken this afternoon rather hard. I'd like to get her home as soon as possible."

"Of course. If there's anything I can do . . ."

"I don't think so." Craig smiled briefly, shook hands and walked briskly away.

Miller watched him until he had disappeared round the side of the church and then he turned and went back to his car.

It was just after ten on the following morning and Max Vernon was having a late breakfast at a small table in front of the fire when there was a knock on the door and Carver came in.

"Now what?" Vernon demanded irritably.

Carver held up a large and very beautiful wreath of white lilies without a word.

"What is it, for God's sake?"

"It's the wreath you told me to get for the Craig girl's funeral. The one I had delivered yesterday. The porter's just found it pinned to the private door in the alley."

"Has he now?" Vernon said softly.

"But that's not all, Max," Carver said. "This came with it."

Vernon took the small pasteboard card that Carver offered and held it up to the light. It was edged in black and the inscription was simple and to the point. *In memory of Maxwell Vernon. 1929—1967. R.I.P.*

CHAPTER 8

Miller came awake slowly and stared up at the ceiling through the early morning gloom. He checked his watch. It was just coming up to six and then he remembered that he was on a rest day. He gave a sigh of pleasure and turned over.

The outside door opened suddenly and as he struggled up on one elbow, there was laughter and the pounding of feet across the floor of the lounge. A moment later, the bedroom door was flung open and his nephews erupted into the room, a large and very eager Airedale leading the way.

The dog scrambled onto the bed and Miller shoved it away with a curse. "Get down, you brute."

Tommy was eight and Roger ten and they moved in on him from both sides gurgling with laughter. "Come on, Uncle Nick, we're taking Fritz to the park for a run."

"Not with me you aren't," Miller said, hitching the blankets over his shoulders.

"Uncle Nick, you promised."

"When?"

"Oh, ages ago."

Fritz leapt clear across the bed and circled the room briskly and Miller sighed. "All right, I know when I'm beaten. But get that brute out of here. You can wait for me in the yard."

After they had gone, he went into the bathroom, splashed cold water on his face and dressed quickly in cord slacks, polo necked sweater and suède boots. He lit a cigarette and went outside.

His brother's house stood in two acres of garden, a large Victorian villa in grey Yorkshire stone, and Miller's flat was above the garage block at the rear. As he went down the fire escape, an engine roared into life inside the garage and the Mini-Cooper reversed into the yard.

Tommy and Fritz were in the rear, Roger at the wheel and Miller opened the door quickly and pushed him into the passenger seat. "Don't you ever let your mother catch you doing that," he said. "You'll get me shot."

When they reached the park, they left the car near the main gates, but instead of going inside, walked down the road to the public playing fields where Miller released Fritz. The Airedale bounded away and the boys ran after him, shouting and laughing.

Miller followed at his own pace, hands in pockets. The morning was cold and grey and yet the wind was bracing and he felt alive again for the first time in weeks.

The boys had reached the line of iron railings that marked the boundary of the park. Suddenly Roger gave a cry that was echoed by Tommy and they disappeared over the skyline.

Miller hurried after them and when he squeezed through a gap in the fence and looked down into the sports arena, a man in a black track suit was running round the grass track, Fritz in hot pursuit. Roger and Tommy were hopping about in the centre calling ineffectually.

By the time Miller reached the bottom of the hill the runner had secured a grip on Fritz's collar and was leading him to the boys. They stood together in a little group and Miller heard a burst of laughter.

"Sorry about that," he said as he approached.

The man in the track suit turned and grinned. "Surprise, surprise." It was Duncan Craig.

"You're right, it is," Miller said. "You're up early."

"The best part of the day. Besides I like to keep fit." He ruffled Roger's hair. "These two imps yours?"

"My nephews," Miller said. "For my sins. Roger and Tommy. Boys, this is Colonel Craig."

They were enormously impressed. "Were you in the war?" Roger demanded.

Craig grinned. "I'm afraid so."

"Commandos?"

"Nothing so romantic."

They looked disappointed and Miller snapped the lead to Fritz's collar. "Don't you believe him. Colonel Craig was something a whole lot more romantic than any commando."

Craig glanced sharply at him. "Been doing a little research, sergeant?"

"You could say that." Miller brought Fritz to heel and nodded to the boys. "We'd better be getting back."

They turned and ran across the arena and Miller nodded to Craig. "I'll be seeing you."

"I'm sure you will."

When he reached the top of the hill, the boys were waiting for him and Miller paused to catch his breath. Below, Craig was already half-way round the track.

"I say, Uncle Nick," Roger said, "he certainly likes running, doesn't he?"

"I suppose he does," Miller said, a slight frown on his face, and then he smiled. "I don't know about you two, but I'm starving. Come on, I'll race you to the car."

Their excited laughter mingled with the dog's barking died into the distance and below in the silent arena, Duncan Craig started on his second circuit, running strongly.

There was a time when Nick Miller had aspired to a black belt in *karate* or *judo*, but the pressure of work had interfered with that pursuit as it had with so many things. When he entered the premises of the Kardon Judo Centre on the following morning, it was his first visit in a month.

Bert King, the senior instructor, was dressed for the mat, but sat at his desk reading the morning paper, a cup of coffee in his hand. He was a small, shrunken man whose head seemed too big for his body and yet in the *dojo,* he was poetry in motion, a third dan in both *judo* and *aikido.*

"Hello, Mr. Miller, long time no see," he said cheerfully.

"I don't seem to have time to turn round these days," Miller said, "but I've got an hour to spare this morning. Any chance of a private lesson?"

Bert shook his head. "Sorry, I've got a client in the *dojo* now warming up. I was just going to go in."

"Anyone I know?"

"I don't think so, he isn't one of the regulars. A chap called Craig."

Miller paused in the act of lighting a cigarette. "Colonel Duncan Craig?"

"That's right. Do you know him?"

"We've met. Is he any good?"

"You're telling me he is," Bert King said emphatically. "His *aikido* is murder—brown belt standard at least. Maybe even first dan and the strange thing is, he isn't even graded. He's been coming in two hours each day for a fortnight now and it's taking me all my time to hold him, I can tell you."

"Mind if I watch?"

"Help yourself." He moved out of the office, opened the door to the *dojo* and went inside. Miller hesitated for a moment and then followed him.

Craig and King faced each other in the centre of the mat. The Colonel was wearing an old *judogi* and looked fit and active, vibrant with energy like an unexploded time bomb.

"Free practice?" Bert King said.

Craig nodded. "All right by me."

The contest which followed lasted just under fifteen minutes and was one of the finest Miller had seen. When it finished, both men were damp with sweat and Bert King looked shaken for the first time since Miller had known him.

"I must be getting old," he said. "Ten minutes' rest and then we'll brush up on some of the finer points."

"That's fine by me." Craig picked up his towel from the bench to wipe the sweat from his face and noticed Miller in the doorway. "Hello, sergeant, we seem to be running into each other all over the place."

"We'll have to get Sergeant Miller on the mat with you one of these days," Bert said.

Miller shook his head. "No thanks. He's too rich for my blood."

"Don't you believe it," Bert told Craig. "He'll give you a run for your money."

"I'm sure he will." Craig dropped his towel on the bench. "I'll go through a few routines till you're ready, Bert."

There was a full-length mirror on the wall and he stood in front of it and started to practice *karate* kicks, knee raised, flicking each foot forward in turn with lightning speed.

"He's good, isn't he?" Bert King observed.

"Too damned good for comfort," Miller said and he turned and went out quickly, his face grim.

"So he likes to take early morning runs in the park and he's keen on *judo*," Grant said. "So what? Plenty of men of his age like to keep fit. Wish I had the time myself."

"But Duncan Craig is no ordinary man," Miller said. "I've been doing a little research on him. He took a B.Sc. in Electrical Engineering at Leeds University in 1939, joined a tank regiment at the outbreak of war and was captured at Arras when the Panzers broke through in 1940. His grandmother was French and he speaks the language fluently, which

helped when he escaped from prison camp and
walked to Spain. Special Operations Executive re-
cruited him when he got home and dropped him into
France on four separate occasions to organise the
maquis. On his last job, he was betrayed, but managed to slip through the net again. They posted him
to the Middle East after that and he spent the rest of
the war working for the Special Air Service organis-
ing guerrillas in the Cretan Mountains."

"He must have been a pretty hard apple," Grant
observed.

"You're telling me. When the war ended he was
twenty-seven and a Lieutenant-Colonel. D.S.O. and
bar, M.C., Legion of Honour—you name it, he's
got it."

The early March wind drove hail like bullets
against the window of Grant's office and he sighed.
"Look here, Nick, don't you think you're getting
this thing completely out of proportion?"

"Do I hell," Miller said. "Can you imagine a man
like that sitting back while his daughter's murderer
walks the streets a free man?"

"Now you're being melodramatic." Grant shook
his head. "I don't buy this one, Nick. I don't buy it
at all. Not that I don't want you to stop keeping a

fatherly eye on Max Vernon. He'll make his move sooner or later and when he does, I want us to be ready for him. As for Craig—just forget about him."

Miller crumpled the sheet of paper he was holding into a ball of paper and Grant lost his temper. "Just let me put you straight on one or two things before you go. In this town alone crime has quadrupled over the past seven years. We've a clear-up rate for housebreaking of sixteen per cent, the average week in the C.I.D. is seventy hours and you want to waste your time on a thing like this? Go on, get out of here and get on with some work."

Miller went back into the outer office and sat down at his desk. Jack Brady came across, a sympathetic grin on his face, and leaned against the wall as he filled his pipe.

"You did ask for it, you know."

Miller sighed and ran his hands over his face. "I'm right, Jack—I know I am."

"Perhaps you are, but I fail to see what you can do about it until something happens. Did you see that note I left for you?"

"This one?" Miller picked a sheet of paper from his In-tray.

"That's right. It came in half an hour ago. You

did say you wanted to know of anything concerning Chuck Lazer's place, didn't you?"

Miller read the report quickly and then picked up the telephone. "Get me the District Inspector for the R.S.P.C.A." He looked up at Brady. "This could mean trouble."

"That's what I thought."

A voice clicked in on the other end of the wire. "Forbes here."

"Good morning, inspector. Detective Sergeant Miller, Central C.I.D. You've sent us a routine report on two poisoned dogs—Dalmatians. I wonder if you'd mind telling me what happened?"

"We got a call from a Mr. Lazer of the Berkley Club in Cork Square at nine o'clock this morning. He found his dogs dead in the alley at the side of the club. Arsenical poisoning, which was why I reported it."

"Did he have any idea who was responsible?"

"He said very little. He was obviously quite distressed—and I don't blame him. They were beautiful animals."

Miller thanked him and replaced the receiver.

"What do you think," Brady said, "a declaration of war?"

"I should imagine so." Miller stood up and took down his trenchcoat from the stand. "We'd better go round and see if we can damp down this little affair before it bursts into flame."

Chuck Lazer was sitting at the piano in the empty casino, a glass at his elbow. He gave a tired grin when Miller and Brady entered and kept right on playing.

"Bad news travels fast."

"It certainly does," Miller said. "Why didn't you let me know?"

"My affair."

"Not in my book." Miller pulled a chair forward and sat astride it, arms resting on the back. "He's going to squeeze you out, Chuck. This is only the first step."

Lazer shrugged and moved into a pushing, intricate arrangement of *Blue Moon*. "I can look after myself."

"What with—a gun?"

Lazer cracked suddenly and completely. "What in the hell do you expect me to do? Bow out gracefully and let him take over? I've put a lot of sweat into this place, Nick. I run an honest game for a nice class of people, which suits me and suits them. I'm damned if I'm going to let Max Vernon walk all over me."

Miller got to his feet, walked across to one of the green baize tables and picked up a pair of dice. He rattled them in his hand and turned, a frown on his face.

"When do you think they'll start, Jack?"

"Probably tonight if what happened to the dogs is anything to go by," Brady said. "Half a dozen heavies mingling with the regular members, complaining about the service, starting a punch-up or two. The usual pattern. Before you know where you are this place will be as dead as the Empire music hall."

Lazer's face had gone grey and his shoulders sagged as he stopped playing. "Okay—you win. What do I do?"

"You do nothing," Miller said. "Just leave everything to us. What time do you open?"

"Eight o'clock, but things don't really get moving till nine-thirty or ten."

Miller turned to Brady enquiringly. "Feel like a night on the town, Jack?"

"Suits me," Brady grinned. "Naturally I'll expect my chips to be on the house."

Lazer managed a faint smile. "I might as well get ruined that way as the other."

Miller clapped him on the shoulder. "Don't worry, Chuck, we'll have the heavy brigade standing by. Anyone who starts anything tonight is in for the shock of their lives."

On returning to Headquarters, Miller went in to see Grant to report on this latest development and then sat down at his desk and started to work his way through some of the paper that had accumulated in his In-tray. It was just before one and he was thinking about going down to the canteen for a sandwich when the 'phone rang.

It was a woman's voice, cool, assured and faintly familiar. "Detective Sergeant Miller?"

"Speaking."

"Harriet Craig here."

"What can I do for you, Miss Craig?"

"I was wondering if we could have a chat."

"I don't see why not. Are you free this afternoon?"

"No, I'm afraid not, and this evening I'm going to the symphony concert at the George Hall with friends." She hesitated as if slightly uncertain. "It finishes at ten. I could meet you then or would that be too late?"

"Not at all," Miller said. "Shall I pick you up outside?"

"No, I'd rather not if you don't mind. There's a bar in Gascoigne Square—the Romney. Do you know it?"

"I certainly do."

"I'll meet you in the lounge at ten fifteen."

Miller replaced the receiver and stared into space, thinking about Gascoigne Square by night and the lounge bar of the Romney, the neon lights of the Flamingo Club flashing across from the other side.

"And now what's she up to?" he asked himself softly.

CHAPTER 9

The evening started slowly at the Berkley as it did at most gaming clubs, but from eight o'clock on, Miller and Brady waited, sitting in comfort in Chuck Lazer's office, watching the activities in the main casino through a two-way mirror.

Lazer was at the piano as always, working his way through one standard after another, stopping occasionally to chat with a favoured customer. He looked cool and immaculate in a mohair evening suit and showed no sign of strain.

Gradually the numbers built up until most of the tables were surrounded by those who came only to watch and all seats were taken. It was just after nine-thirty when Brady gave a sudden exclamation and touched Miller's sleeve.

"Coming through the door now. The three at the back."

Miller nodded. "I've got them."

"The man at the front is Manchester Charlie Ford, followed by Frank Butcher. I sent him down for G.B.H. once. Three years. The little bloke with hair like patent leather is Sid Tordoff—a right villain."

"They aren't local lads?"

"Are they hell—Manchester. They've been imported specially—probably via a middle man. You know how it goes. A pound to a penny they don't even know who they're working for."

They waited and a few moments later he nodded again. "I thought so. Arthur Hart and Martin Dereham—he's the good-looking one with the buttonhole and the moustache. Tries to come the public school touch, but the highest he ever got up the educational ladder was class four at Dock Street Elementary."

"Okay," Miller said, getting to his feet. "I'm going in. Better put a call through to H.Q. We'll have the heavy brigade standing by just in case."

It was a quiet, well-behaved crowd, mostly mon-eyed people, the kind who'd run for cover and never come back at the slightest hint of violence or trouble of any sort. Miller scanned the faces quickly, noting that the gang had dispersed themselves, which prob-ably indicated outbursts of trouble in several differ-ent places at once.

And then he saw Manchester Charlie Ford on the other side of the roulette wheel. Ford was of medium height with powerful sloping shoulders, the scar tis-sue beneath his eyes indicating that he had once been a prize fighter. He was wearing a surprisingly well-cut suit and pushed his way through the crowd with an arrogance that was obviously beginning to alarm several people.

He paused behind a rather attractive woman. It was impossible to see what actually happened, but she turned sharply and her escort, a dark-haired young man, rounded on Ford. "What's the game?"

So this was how it was to start? Miller slipped through the crowd, arriving from the rear, and se-cured a grip on Ford's left wrist before he knew what had hit him.

"Get moving!" he said softly into Ford's ear. "Try anything funny and I'll break your arm."

Before the young couple could say a word, Miller and Ford had been swallowed up by the crowd. They came to rest behind a pillar, Miller still retaining his grip. Ford's right hand dived into his pocket. As it came out again, Jack Brady arrived on the scene and relieved him of a wicked-looking spiked knuckle-duster.

"Well, well, if it isn't my old friend Manchester Charlie Ford."

Ford looked ready to commit murder and when Miller turned and glanced over the crowd, he saw the others making rapidly for the exit.

"Are they leaving you then, Charlie?" Brady said. "Isn't that a shame?"

They hustled him into Lazer's office between them and Miller shoved him down into a chair. "Who's paying the piper on this little caper?"

"Why don't you get knotted?" Ford said.

Brady dangled the knuckle-duster in front of him between thumb and forefinger. "Carrying an offensive weapon, Charlie, and with your record? Good for six months that."

"I can do that standing on my head." Ford turned as Lazer entered the room, a worried look on his face. "Are you Lazer?" He laughed harshly. "Had to bring in the bloody scuffers, eh? That's your lot, boyo. I hope you realise that. You're dead meat."

"Why don't you shut up?" Miller said and glanced at his watch. "I'll have to go, Jack. I've got a date. Will you book him for me?"

"My pleasure."

Brady yanked Ford to his feet and took him out through the side door and Miller turned to Lazer. "Don't take any notice of that goon, Chuck. We've made a good start. They'll think twice the next time."

"Oh, sure—sure they will," Lazer said, but his eyes were unhappy and Miller knew that he didn't believe him for a moment.

The lounge bar of the Romney was only half full when Miller entered shortly after ten, but there was no sign of Harriet Craig. He sat on a stool at the end of the bar, ordered a brandy and ginger ale and lit a cigarette. When he glanced up, he could see her in the mirror standing in the doorway behind him.

She was wearing an evening coat in green grosgraine which hung open at the front to reveal a simple black cocktail dress and when she smiled on catching sight of him, she looked quite enchanting.

"Am I late?" she asked as she sat on the stool beside him.

"No, I was early. How about a drink?"

"Please. A dry martini."

"How was the concert?"

"Fine—Mendelssohn's *Ruy Blas* and a Mozart piano concerto. Do you like classical music?"

"Some—I'm a jazz man myself. How's your father?"

"Fine—just fine." She stared down into her glass and sighed. "Look, I'm afraid I've rather got you here under false pretences."

"You mean you don't want to chat after all?"

She nodded. "As a matter of fact I was hoping you might take me out."

"Now there's an attractive idea," he said. "Where would you like to go?"

"I'd like to go to the Flamingo."

"May I ask why?"

"Those murals Joanna painted for Vernon—I'd like to see them. The only other way would be to ask his permission and I'd hate that." She opened her bag and took out a gold-edged card. "I've got a membership card—one of Daddy's business friends arranged it for me and members are allowed to take guests in with them."

Miller sat there looking down at the card for a long moment, a slight frown on his face and she put a hand on his arm. "Please, Nick? I'd feel safe with you."

"You make a very appealing liar," Miller said, "but I'll still take you. In fact I wouldn't miss it for the world. I'm sure it will prove more than interesting."

The Flamingo had altered a lot since Miller's last visit, but that had been in the old days when Harry Faulkner had owned it and it had been more a night club than anything else, with gambling relegated to a strictly illegal small back room. The Gaming Act had changed all that and now there was money to burn.

The small, thickly carpeted foyer had been decorated in excellent taste and the man who moved forward to check Harriet's membership card was greying and distinguished and wore hunting pink. They went through a door at the end of a short passage and found themselves at the top of a flight of steps which dropped into the main casino.

"Oh, look, Nick! Look!" Harriet clutched at his arm.

The murals were astonishingly good. There were four of them in enormous panels, two on either side of the long room. They were all battle scenes, the Foot Guards figuring largely in each one, and had been executed in a rather stylistic seventeenth-century manner and yet had a life and originality that was all their own.

Miller shook his head slowly. "I just didn't realise she was that good."

"She could have been a great painter, Nick," Harriet said. "Something special." She took a deep breath and smiled as though determined to be cheerful. "Well, as long as we're here we might as well have a look round."

There were the usual games—Chemmy, Roulette, Blackjack and, in a small side room, Poker was on offer. But it was the clientele which Miller found most interesting. There was little doubt that Vernon was catering for the top people with a vengeance. The kind of money being wagered would have been sufficient to indicate that, but in any case, Miller recognised faces here and there. Wool barons, industrialists, the managing director of one of the world's

largest ready-made clothing factories. There were at
least four millionaires present to his personal knowledge.

The whole place had the atmosphere of a West-
End club, only a low buzz of conversation disturbed
the silence and grave-faced waiters in hunting pink
moved from table to table dispensing free drinks.

Manchester Charlie Ford and his boys would never
have got past the door, but if they had, they would
have closed the place down by just one visit. With the
kind of clientele it catered for, a club like the Flamingo
depended on its reputation. Take that away from it
and it was finished.

They stood by the roulette wheel watching the
play and she turned suddenly. "I'd like to have a go.
What do I do?"

"Decide how much you can afford to lose, that's
lesson number one."

She opened her handbag and produced two five-
pound notes. "Will this be all right?"

He grinned. "It won't go far in a place like this,
but never mind. Who knows? You may even break the
bank. Wait here, I'll get you some chips."

.   .   .

Max Vernon sat at his desk, magnificent in a midnight blue dinner jacket, a white gardenia in his buttonhole. For supper, the chef had presented him with a mixed grill done to perfection and a glass of champagne was at his elbow.

The man who stood on the other side of the desk, an open ledger in his hand, was Claudio Carelli, the casino manager, and he looked worried.

"But it isn't good, Mr. Vernon. We put a lot of money into this place. The new décor and refurnishing came to twenty-two thousand and then there are the running expenses. At the moment, we're virtually living from day to day."

"You worry too much, Claudio," Vernon said. "It takes time to build up a prestige club like this. But they're coming now—all the right people. Another three months and we'll be in the clear."

"I certainly hope so."

As Carelli opened the door to leave, Stratton came in, his face pale with excitement. "Miller's downstairs in the casino."

"How did he get in?"

"He's with the Craig girl. Ben saw them come in. He checked with Bruno on the door. She's a member all right, everything square and above board. She brought Miller in as her guest."

"Who put her up?"

"Bruno says it was Sir Frank Wooley. Shall we get rid of them?"

"You bloody fool." Vernon reached across the desk and grabbed him by the tie. "How many times have I got to tell you? No trouble in the club. What do you want to do—bankrupt me?" He shoved Stratton away from him and poured another glass of champagne. "Keep an eye on them. I'll be down myself in ten minutes."

Harriet had a small, but exciting run of luck at Roulette that took her up to seventy pounds.

"I think I'd better try something else while I'm ahead," she said. "What are they playing over there?"

"One of the oldest games of chance in the world," Miller told her. "You simply throw the dice and pray that the right number comes up."

"Any skill required?"

"Not to my knowledge."

"Then that's the game for me."

The table was a popular one and not only were all the seats taken, but a fair-sized crowd stood around watching. Harriet had to wait for five minutes before her chance came. The first time she threw, she didn't cast the dice far enough and the croupier handed them back to her with a whispered instruction. There were one or two good-humoured remarks and then she made two straight passes and doubled her money.

There were encouraging smiles from the crowd and she laughed excitedly. "These dice can't possibly have any more luck in them. Can I have a new pair?"

"Certainly, madame."

The croupier passed them across and removed the others. Harriet rattled the dice in one hand and threw a pair of ones. "Snakes' eyes," said a military-looking gentleman with a curving moustache who was standing next to her. "Bad luck."

She tried again with no better luck and the third throw cleaned her out. "How strange," she said with a little laugh. "I just keep getting a pair of ones, don't I?"

"The luck of the game, my dear," the military-looking man said.

She picked up the dice and rolled them gently no more than a foot or so. "Look, there they are again. It just isn't my night."

The croupier's rake reached out, but the military

man beat him to it, a frown on his face. "Not so fast there."

"I hope monsieur is not suggesting that there could be anything wrong with the dice?"

"We'll see, shall we?"

He rattled the dice together and threw them the length of the table. *Snakes' eyes.* The croupier's rake moved out, but the military man beat him to it again. "Oh, no you don't, my friend. These dice are loaded." There was a sudden hubbub amongst the crowd and he turned to an elderly, white-haired man at his side. "See for yourself."

The elderly man tossed the dice across the table and the result was plain for all to see. Voices were raised suddenly, people got up from other tables and came across as the news spread like wildfire.

Harriet Craig moved through the crowd to Miller's side. "They *are* getting excited, aren't they?"

Before he could reply, Vernon appeared on the scene, pushing his way through the crowd, his face angry. "What's going on here?"

"I was just going to ask you the same question, Vernon," the white-haired man said. "To start with you'll oblige me by throwing these dice."

Vernon stood there, holding them in his hand, a

bewildered frown on his face and then he threw. There was a roar from the crowd and the white-haired man gathered them up quickly.

"That settles it. Somebody better get the police." He turned and addressed the crowd. "I don't know about the rest of you, but I've dropped four hundred pounds here during the past couple of weeks and I'm not leaving till I get it back."

"Ladies and gentlemen—please." Vernon raised his arms in an attempt to placate them, but it was no use.

The voices rose angrily on either side and Miller pushed his way forward and tapped the white-haired man on the shoulder. "I think I'd better have those, sir."

"And who the devil might you be?"

"Detective Sergeant Miller, Central C.I.D." Miller produced his warrant and the dice were passed over without a murmur.

Miller looked across at Vernon. "Are these your dice, sir?"

"Of course not."

"I notice that in accordance with a specific regulation of the Gaming Act, they carry this club's registered mark as placed there by the makers. What you are saying is that you have a full set without this pair? That these are forgeries?"

"But that's rubbish," the white-haired man put in. "What on earth would be the point of a player substituting for the real dice a pair that would make him lose every time he threw."

Vernon's shoulders sagged and his knuckles gleamed whitely as he gripped the edge of the table. He glared across at Miller, who returned his stare calmly.

"Right—I think that's it for tonight, Mr. Vernon."

"What in hell do you mean?" Vernon demanded furiously.

"I mean that I'm closing you up."

"Yes, closing you up for good, you damned crook," the white-haired man said, leaning across the table.

For a moment, Vernon gazed wildly about him and then he turned, pushed his way through the crowd and disappeared upstairs.

It was just after eleven when Miller went down the Town Hall steps to the Cooper. The radio was playing faintly and when he opened the door, Harriet

Craig sat in the passenger seat, humming softly to herself.

"All finished?" she said brightly.

Her handbag was at her feet and he picked it up without answering and searched it quickly.

"What on earth are you looking for?"

"The other pair of dice—the ones you palmed. Where are they?"

"I haven't the slightest idea what you're talking about."

Miller tossed the handbag into her lap, switched on the engine and drove away. "I don't like being used."

"Not even in a good cause?"

"For God's sake, Harriet, don't you realise what you've done? You've finished the Flamingo. An exclusive gaming house lives on its reputation. All it takes is one tiny scandal—just one and the clientele disappear like the snow in the springtime."

"Poor Mr. Vernon. What rotten luck."

"If you imagine for one moment he's going to take it lying down, you've got another thought coming."

"We'll see, shall we?" She settled back in her seat, arms folded and sighed. "Those murals were wonderful—really wonderful. Who knows? Maybe he'll be willing to sell them now."

"You'll come in for a drink?" she said when they reached the house.

"Are you sure it isn't too late?"

"Of course not. We'll have something to eat if you like. I'm starving."

She unlocked the front door and led the way into the hall and Miller was at once aware of the low persistent hum of a dynamo. "Daddy must still be working," she said. "Come on. I'll take you through to the workshop. You two can chat while I make some supper."

When she opened the door at the end of the corridor Miller paused in astonishment. The room had been expertly equipped and fitted, of that there could be no doubt. The walls were lined with shelves which seemed to carry just about every kind of spare imaginable in the electrical field. There was an automatic lathe, a cutter and several other machines whose purpose was a complete mystery to him.

Duncan Craig leaned over a bench, spot-welding

a length of steel rod to what looked like the insides of a computer. He glanced up as the door opened, killed the flame on the blow torch and pushed up his goggles.

"Hello there," he said. "And what have you two been up to?"

"Nick took me to the Flamingo," Harriet said. "Quite an experience, but I'll tell you all about it later. Keep him occupied while I get the supper."

The door closed behind her and Craig offered Miller a cigarette. "She seems to have enjoyed herself."

"How could she fail to? Seeing Max Vernon fall flat on his face must have quite made her day."

Craig's expression didn't alter. "Oh, yes, what happened then?"

"Apparently the casino was using crooked dice. There was quite a fuss when it was discovered."

"My God, I bet there was." Craig contrived to look shocked. "This won't do Vernon much good, will it?"

"He might as well close up shop. There'll be a prosecution of course, but even if it doesn't get anywhere, the damage is done."

"How did he react?"

"Oh, he said he'd been framed. That the loaded dice must have been passed by one of the players."

"But that's ridiculous," Craig said. "I could imagine a player trying to substitute dice that would win for him, but not a pair that would lose. Anyway, a club's dice have to be specially manufactured and accounted for. It's a regulation of the Gaming Act expressly aimed at stamping out this sort of thing."

Miller moved along the bench and picked up a small stick of lead. "Easy enough for a man with some technical know-how to inject a little lead into a pair of plastic dice."

"But what would be the point of the exercise?"

"I think that's been achieved, don't you?"

"Well, I'm hardly likely to shed tears over Max Vernon, am I?"

"I suppose not."

Miller wandered round the bench and paused beside a curious contrivance—a long, chromium tube mounted on a tripod. It had a pistol grip at one end and what appeared to be a pair of small headphones clipped to a hook.

"What's this—a secret weapon?"

Craig chuckled. "Hardly—it's a directional microphone."

Miller was immediately interested. "I've heard of those. How do they work?"

"It's a simple electronic principle. The tube is lined with carbon to exclude side noises, traffic for instance. You aim it by ear through the headphones. It can pick up a conversation three hundred yards away."

"Is that so?"

"Of course these are even handier." He picked up a small metal disk that was perhaps half an inch thick and little larger than a wrist watch. "Not only a microphone but also a radio transmitter. Works well up to a range of a hundred yards or so if you use a fountain pen receiver. Wire that up to a pocket tape recorder and you're in business."

"What as?" Miller asked.

"That depends on the individual, doesn't it?"

"I suppose you're aware that all these gadgets are illegal?"

"Not for the Managing Director of Gulf Electronics."

Miller shook his head. "You're a fool, colonel. Carry on like this and you'll be in trouble up to your neck."

"I don't know what you're talking about." Craig

smiled blandly. "By the way, harking back to what you said earlier about doctoring the dice. One would have to get hold of them first."

"Easy enough to get into a place like the Flamingo, especially in the small hours just after they've closed."

"I should have thought that might have presented some difficulty."

"Not for the kind of man who broke into a Vichy prison in 1942 and spirited away four resistance workers who were due to be executed next morning."

Craig laughed. "Now you're flattering me."

"Warning you," Miller said grimly. "It's got to stop. Carry on like this and you'll go too far and no one will be able to help you—just remember that."

"Oh, I will," Craig said, his smile still hooked firmly into place.

"Good." Miller opened the door. "Tell Harriet I'm sorry, but I've suddenly lost my appetite."

The door closed behind him. Craig's smile disappeared instantly. He stood there staring into space for a while, then pulled down his goggles, re-lit the blow torch and started to work again.

· · ·

Max Vernon walked to the fireplace and back to his desk again, restless as a caged tiger, and Carver and Stratton watched him anxiously.

"This is serious," he said. "Don't you stupid bastards realise that? One single scandal—that's all you need in a prestige club like this and you're finished. My God, did you see their faces? They'll never come back."

"Maybe things aren't as bad as you think, Mr. Vernon," Carver ventured and Vernon turned on him.

"You bloody fool, we've been living from day to day, waiting for things to build up. I've been using the take from the Flamingo to keep the betting shops running. Now what happens?"

He sat down behind his desk and poured himself a brandy. "Who's done this to me—who?"

"Maybe it was Chuck Lazer," Stratton suggested.

"Do me a favour?" Vernon drained his glass. "I know one thing. Whoever it is will wish he'd never been born before I'm through with him."

He slammed his fist down hard on the desk and something dropped to the floor and rolled across the carpet. Vernon leaned over and frowned. "What was that?"

Stratton picked up the small steel disk and passed it over. "Search me, Mr. Vernon. It fell off the desk when you hit it. Must have been underneath."

Vernon stared down incredulously and then grabbed a paper knife and forced off the top. "I've seen one of these before," he said. "It's an electronic gadget—a microphone and transmitter." His face was suddenly distorted with fury and he dropped the disk on the floor and ground his heel into it. "We've been wired for sound. Some bastard's been listening in."

He reached for the brandy bottle and paused, eyes narrowing. "Just a minute—Craig's Managing Director of an electronics firm, isn't he?"

Stratton nodded eagerly. "That's right and his daughter was here tonight remember."

"So she was," Vernon said softly. "Plus that nosy copper, Miller. Come to think of it, that's twice he's stuck his nose into my business in one night. That won't do—that won't do at all."

"Do you want Ben and me to handle it?" Stratton said.

Vernon shook his head and poured himself another glass of brandy. "Not on your life. Contract it out, Billy. A couple of real pros should be enough. One of the south London mobs might be interested.

Just make sure they don't know who they're working for, that's all."

"How much can I offer?" Stratton asked.

"Five hundred."

"For Craig?" Stratton's eyes widened. "That's a good price, Mr. Vernon."

"For both of them, you fool. Miller and Craig." Vernon raised his glass of brandy in an ironic salute. "Down the hatch," he said and smiled grimly.

CHAPTER 10

It was dark in the office except for the pool of light falling across the drawing board from the anglepoise lamp. Duncan Craig put down his slide-rule and stretched with a sigh. It was almost eight o'clock and for the past two hours he had worked on alone after the rest of his staff had left.

There were footsteps in the corridor and as he turned, the door opened and the night guard entered, a black and tan Alsatian on a lead at his side. He put a thermos flask on the desk and grinned.

"Just checking, colonel. I've brought you a cup of tea."

"Thanks very much, George." Craig ruffled the

dog's ears. "What time's your next round—nine o'clock isn't it?"

"That's right, sir. Will you still be here?"

"The way this thing is going I'll probably be here all night."

The door closed behind George and Craig stood there listening to his footsteps move along the corridor outside. When they had finally faded away, he went into the washroom quickly and closed the door.

When he reappeared five minutes later he presented a strange and sinister picture in dark pants and sweater, and wearing an old balaclava helmet, his face darkened by a brown make-up stick. In his left hand he carried a canvas hold-all. He dropped it on the floor beside his desk, picked up the telephone and dialled a number.

The receiver was lifted instantly at the other end. "Yes?"

"I'm leaving. I'll ring you again in thirty-five minutes."

"I'll be waiting."

He replaced the receiver, picked up the hold-all and opened the door, listening for a moment before moving into the corridor.

He took the service lift down to the basement,

walked through the work's garage, helping himself to a jerry can full of petrol on the way, and left through a small judas gate. It was raining slightly and he crossed the yard, keeping to the shadows, scrambled over the low wall and dropped down onto the grass bank that sloped into the canal.

He crouched at the water's edge, opened the hold-all and pulled out the collapsible dinghy it contained. When he activated the compression cylinder, the boat inflated with a soft hiss and he dropped it into the water and pushed off into the darkness.

He'd kept Gibson's Furniture Factory under careful observation for three days now from the top floor of his own factory, even going to the lengths of obtaining a ground-floor plan of the place from the City Engineer's Department, for most of the area was scheduled for demolition and municipal development.

It was no more than four hundred yards up the York Road from Gulf Electronics and an approach from the rear via the canal had seemed obvious. He grinned as he paddled out into mid-stream to pass the barge and moved back into the shadows again. Just like the old days—other times, other places when to live a life like this had seemed as natural as breathing.

He passed the coaling wharf of the steel plant, dark and lonely in the light of a solitary yellow lamp. The furniture factory was the second building along from there and he paddled in quickly, scrambled out onto a narrow strip of mud and pulled the dinghy clear.

The brick wall above his head was about nine feet high, but old and crumbling and in spite of being encumbered with the jerry can he found no difficulty in scaling it. For a moment he sat there peering into the darkness and then dropped into the yard below.

A light glowed dimly through the dirty windows and he moved round to the front of the building keeping to the shadows. The whole area was enclosed by a crumbling brick wall. The main gates were of wood, ten feet high and secured by a massive iron bar which dropped into sockets on either side.

In one corner of the yard was a jumbled mass of packing cases and rubbish which had obviously accumulated over the years and it was for this that he had brought the petrol. He emptied the jerry can quickly, scattering its contents as widely as possible, and then returned to the gates and removed the holding bar.

He checked his watch. It was exactly fifteen

minutes since he had left his office. From now on, speed was essential.

He hit his first snag when he reached the main door of the factory. It was locked. He hesitated only for a moment and then tried his alternative route up an old fire escape to the second floor. The door at the top was also locked, but several panes of glass in the window beside it were broken and it opened with little difficulty.

He stood in the darkness listening, aware of voices somewhere in the distance, and moved along a short corridor. There was a door at the end with a broken panel through which light streamed. He opened it cautiously and was at once aware of a strong smell of whisky.

He was on a steel landing. The hall below was crowded with crates, and a large six-wheeler truck, which certainly didn't look as if it belonged, was parked a yard or two away from the main doors.

The voices came from his left and he went along the landing, passing a small glass-walled office which stood in darkness. There was a light in a room at the very end of the landing and he peered round the edge of the glass partition and found three men playing poker.

He withdrew quietly, went back along the landing and descended the iron stairs to the hall below. The truck was loaded with crates of whisky consigned to London Docks and when he looked inside the cab, the ignition key was in the dashboard.

The main doors were the real snag. They were chained together and secured by a large padlock. He examined it carefully, turned and went back upstairs.

He crouched in the darkness of the little office, the 'phone on the floor beside him, and dialled the number he wanted carefully.

The reply was instant. "Police Headquarters. Can I help you?"

"Central C.I.D.—Detective Sergeant Miller," Craig said in a hoarse voice. "I think you'll find he's on duty tonight."

Miller was sitting behind his desk listening to a well-known housebreaker indignantly deny the offence with which he was charged when the 'phone rang.

"All right, Arnold, you can take a breather," he said and nodded to Brady, who leaned against the wall cleaning his fingernails with a penknife. "Give him a cigarette, Jack, while I see what we've got here."

He picked up the telephone. "Detective Sergeant Miller."

The voice at the other end was strangely hoarse and completely unfamiliar to him. "Gibson's Furniture Factory on the York Road—interesting place— they even make their own booze. You'd better get round here quick and bring the Fire Brigade with you." He chuckled harshly. "I do hope Vernon's insured."

Craig replaced the receiver and looked at the luminous dial of his watch. He was running late, but there was nothing he could do about that now. He waited exactly four minutes, went back downstairs and climbed into the cab of the truck.

He pulled out the choke, pressed the starter and the engine burst into life with a shattering roar. There was a cry of alarm from the landing above his head and he rammed the stick into first gear, let in the clutch sharply and accelerated. The doors burst open and the truck rolled out into the yard. Craig swerved sharply, braking to a halt near the outside gates, switched off and jumped to the ground taking the ignition key with him.

He struck a match quickly and tossed it onto the stacked crates, picked up his jerry can, turned and ran into the shadows. Somewhere in the night, the jangle of a police car's bell sounded ominously.

When he drifted into the side of the canal below the wall of his own factory yard five minutes later, there was already a considerable disturbance in the vicinity of the furniture factory and a red glow stained the darkness, flames leaping into the night from the stack of burning crates.

He took a knife from his pocket and slashed the dinghy in several places, forcing out all air so that he was able to stuff it into the hold-all again, then he tossed it over the wall with the jerry can and followed them.

He left the can with a stack of similar ones on his way through the garage and returned to the tenth floor in the service lift. The moment he was safely inside his office, he reached for the 'phone and dialled his home. As before, the receiver was lifted instantly at the other end.

"You're late," Harriet said.

"Sorry about that. I must be getting old."

She chuckled. "That'll be the day. Everything go off okay?"

"Couldn't be better. I won't be home just yet, by

the way. I want to finish the details on the vibrator modification in time for the staff conference tomorrow."

"How long will you be?"

"Another couple of hours should do it."

"I'll have some supper waiting."

He replaced the receiver, went into the washroom, scrubbed the filth from his body and changed quickly. He had hardly returned to the other room when there was a knock on the door and George came in.

"Hell of a fuss going on up the road, sir. Don't know what it's all about, but everybody seems to be there. Fire, police—the lot."

"Go and have a look if you like," Craig said.

"Sure you don't mind, sir?"

"Not at all. I'd be interested to know what's happening myself."

He sat down at the drawing board and picked up his slide-rule and George went out quickly.

Miller and Grant stood by the ashes of the fire and surveyed the scene. The Fire Brigade had left, but the big black van that was known throughout the Department as the Studio was parked just inside the gates and the boys from Forensic were already getting to work on the truck.

"So no one was around when the first car got here?" Grant asked, for he had only just arrived on the scene and was seeking information.

"That's right, sir. Whoever was here must have cleared off pretty sharpish. Of course the fire was bound to attract attention."

"What about the truck?"

"Hi-jacked two days ago on the A1 near Wetherby. Carrying a consignment of export Scotch to the London Docks. Valued at £30,000."

Grant whistled softly. "That's going to bring the county's crime figures down a bit. And you say you didn't recognise the informer's voice?" he added incredulously.

"I'm afraid not."

"Well, all I can say is you've got a good snout there, by God."

Jack Brady emerged from the factory and came towards them, an open document in one hand. "We've found the lease on this place in a filing cabinet in the office, sir," he said. "It's made out in the name of Frank O'Connor. The property's been made the subject of a demolition order so it's owned by the city. O'Connor's a citizen of Eire by the way."

"And probably on his way back there as fast as he can run at this very moment," Grant observed and turned to Miller. "You're sure the snout mentioned Vernon's name?"

"Absolutely."

"Doesn't make sense then, does it?"

"It does if O'Connor was just a front man."

"I suppose so. Just try proving that and see where it gets you. I know one thing—if it is Vernon's place then someone certainly has it in for him." He glanced at his watch. "My God, it's almost eleven. Too late for me. See you two in the morning."

He moved away and Brady turned to Miller. "Ready to go, Nick? Not much more we can do here."

"You know, Grant's right," Miller said. "Whoever set this little lot up for us must really have it in for Vernon. Hang on a minute. I want to make a 'phone call."

"Checking on someone?"

"That's right—Duncan Craig."

"Not that again, Nick," Brady groaned. "Why don't you leave it alone?"

Miller ignored him and went to the 'phone box on the corner. Harriet Craig sounded cool and impersonal. "Harriet Craig speaking."

"Nick Miller."

"Hello, Nick." There was a new warmth in her voice. "When are you coming round to finish your supper?"

"Almost any day now. I'm just waiting for the crime figures to fall. Is your father in? I'd like a word with him."

"I'm sorry, he isn't. He's working late tonight. Was it important?"

"Not really. I've got a rest day Saturday and I thought he might be interested in a game of golf."

"I'm sure he would. Shall I tell him to give you a call?"

"Yes, you do that. I'll have to go now, Harriet, we're having a hard night."

"Poor Nick." She laughed. "Don't forget to keep in touch."

"How could I?"

He replaced the receiver and went back to Brady.

"Now there's a thing—guess where Craig is at this very moment? Working late at the factory."

"Gulf Electronics is only just down the road," Brady said. "The big new block. You can see it from here. There's a light in one of the top-floor offices."

As Miller turned, the light went out. "Let's take a look."

"Suit yourself," Brady said as they moved to the car. "But I think you're making a big mistake."

As they drove away there was a low rumble of thunder in the distance and quite suddenly, the light rain which had been falling steadily for the past hour turned into a solid driving downpour. The main gates of Gulf Electronics stood open and Miller pulled into the side of the road and switched off.

At the same moment, the glass entrance doors opened and Duncan Craig appeared, the night guard at his side with the Alsatian.

"That's old George Brown," Brady said. "Sergeant in 'B' Division for years. Got himself a nice touch there."

Brown went back inside, locking the doors, and Craig stood at the top of the steps, belting his raincoat and pulling on his gloves. He turned up his collar, went down the steps and hurried into the darkness of the car park. A second later, two men moved out of the shadows at the side of the door and went after him.

"I don't like the look of that one little bit," Miller said, wrenching open the door. "Come on!"

He turned in through the gates, running hard, and from somewhere in the darkness of the car park there came a scream.

Duncan Craig had almost reached his car when he heard the rush of feet through the darkness behind and swung round. A fist lifted into his face as he ducked and he staggered back against the car, flinging himself to one side. One of his assailants raised an iron bar two-handed above his head and brought it down with such force that he dented the roof of the Jaguar.

A razor gleamed in the diffused light from the street lamps on the other side of the railings and he warded off the descending blow with a left block, and kicked the man sharply in the stomach so that he screamed in agony.

There was another rush of feet through the darkness and Miller and Brady arrived. The man with the iron bar started to turn and Brady delivered a beautiful right to the jaw that had all his fourteen stone behind it.

There was a sudden silence and Craig laughed. "Right on time. I don't know what I'd have done without you."

Miller snapped the cuffs on the man who was lying on the ground and hauled him to his feet. "Anyone you know, Jack?"

Brady held the other one against Craig's car. "They're not off our patch, that's certain. Specially imported I shouldn't wonder."

Miller turned on Craig savagely. "Maybe you'll listen to reason from now on." He sent his prisoner staggering into the darkness in front of him. "Come on, Jack, let's take them in."

Craig stood there in the darkness without moving until the Cooper had driven away and then he unlocked the door of the Jaguar and climbed behind the driving wheel. He knew something was wrong the moment she refused to start. He tried several times ineffectually, then took a flashlight from the glove compartment, got out and raised the bonnet. The rotor arm had been removed, an obvious precaution in case he'd beaten them into the car. He sighed heavily, dropped the bonnet and moved across to the main gates.

It was only twenty past eleven and there were plenty of late buses about, but in any case, he would be able to get a taxi in City Square. He crossed the road quickly, head down against the driving rain.

Someone moved out of a doorway behind him, he was aware of that, and then the pain as a sharp point sliced through his raincoat and jacket to touch bare flesh.

"Keep walking," Billy Stratton said calmly. "Just keep walking or I'll shove this right through your kidneys."

They turned into a narrow alley a few yards further along, Craig walking at the same even pace, hands thrust deep into his pockets. A lamp was bracketed to the wall at the far end and beyond, the river roared over a weir, drowning every other sound.

"A good thing I came along, wasn't it?" Stratton said. "But then I have an instinct for these things. I knew something would go wrong just as I knew you were trouble from the first moment I clapped eyes on you. But not any more, you bastard. Not any more."

Craig took to his heels and ran and Stratton cried

out in fury and went after him. The cobbles at the end of the alley were black and shiny in the light of the old gas lamp and beyond the low wall that blocked the end, the river rushed through the darkness.

As Craig turned, Stratton paused, the knife held ready, a terrible grin splitting the white face, and then he moved with incredible speed, the blade streaking up. To Duncan Craig, it might have been a branch swaying in the breeze. He pivoted cleanly to one side, secured the wrist in a terrible *aikido* grip and twisted the hand back in the one way nature had never intended it should go, snapping the wrist instantly.

Stratton screamed soundlessly, his agony drowned by the roaring of the river. He staggered back clutching his broken wrist, mouthing obscenities, and as Craig picked up the knife and moved towards him, turned and stumbled away.

Craig went after him, but Stratton thundered along the alley as if all the devils in hell were at his heels, emerged into the main road and ran headlong into the path of a late-night bus.

There was a squeal of brakes as the bus skidded, a sudden cry and then silence. A moment later voices were raised and when Craig reached the end of the alley, passengers were already beginning to dismount, men crouching down to peer under the wheels.

"Oh, my God, look at him!" A woman sobbed suddenly and Craig turned up his collar and walked away quickly through the heavy rain.

CHAPTER 11

The disk shot high into the air, poised for one split second at the high point of its trajectory and disintegrated, the sound of the gunshot reverberating through the quiet morning.

The rooks lifted into the air from their nests in the beech trees at the end of the garden, crying in alarm, and Duncan Craig laughed and lowered the automatic shotgun.

"I'm not too popular, it would seem. Let's have another."

As Harriet leaned over the firer to insert another disk, Jenny came out through the French windows.

"There's a gentleman to see you, Colonel Craig. A Mr. Vernon."

Craig paused in the act of reloading the Gower and turned to Harriet, who straightened slowly. "Does he now?" he said softly. "All right, Jenny, show him out here."

Harriet came to him quickly, anxiety on her face, and he slipped an arm about her shoulders. "Don't get alarmed. There's nothing to worry about. Not a damned thing. Let's have another one."

The disk soared into the air and this time he caught it on the way down, a difficult feat at the best of times, snap-shooting from the shoulder, scattering the fragments across the lawn.

"Am I supposed to be impressed?" Vernon said and Craig turned to find him standing in the French windows, Ben Carver at his shoulder.

"Well, well, if it isn't Mr. Vernon," Craig said. "And to what do we owe the honour?"

Vernon nodded towards Harriet. "What about her?"

Craig smiled faintly. "Anything you say to me, you say to Harriet. She's my right arm."

Vernon took a cigarette from a platinum case and Carver gave him a light. "All right, colonel, I'll put my cards on the table. I made a mistake about you, that I freely admit, but I know when I'm beaten."

"I wish I knew what you were talking about," Craig said.

Vernon obviously had difficulty in restraining himself. "Let's stop beating about the bush. I've lost the Flamingo and my place up the York Road and then Billy Stratton meets with a nasty accident. You aren't going to tell me I'm just experiencing a run of bad luck?"

"It can happen to the best of us."

"All right—I'll lay it on the line. You've had your fun—you've broken me, so I'm getting out just as soon as I can find a buyer for what's left. I'm asking you to leave it alone from now on—all right?"

"Oh, no, Mr. Vernon," Craig said softly. "Not in a thousand years. I'll see you in hell first and that's a very definite promise."

"That's all I wanted to know." Far from being angry Vernon now smiled amiably. "You're being very silly, old man. I mean it isn't as if you've only got yourself to consider, is it? There's Harriet here . . ."

He got no further. There was an ominous click and the barrel of the shotgun swung round to touch his chest. Craig's eyes seemed to look right through him and the voice was cold and hard.

"If you even try, Vernon, I'll shoot you down like a dog. In your own home, in the street—you'll never know when it's coming—never feel safe again."

For a long moment Vernon held his gaze and then quite suddenly he nodded to Carver. "Let's go."

They walked across the lawn and disappeared round the side of the house. Harriet moved to her father's side. "Why did he come?"

"For another look at the opposition I think. Nothing like knowing the enemy—a cardinal rule of war and Vernon was a good officer, make no mistake about that."

"But what was the point of all that business about selling out and asking you to lay off?"

"Who knows? It might have worked—perhaps that's what he was hoping. He may even be up to something." Duncan Craig smiled. "We'll have to find out, won't we?"

"What now, Mr. Vernon?" Ben Carver said as he turned the Rolls into the main road.

"We'll go back to the club," Vernon told him.

"After lunch I want you to drive down to Doncaster to pick up Joe Morgan. I told him to leave the London train there just in case."

"Do I bring him back to the Flamingo?"

Vernon shook his head. "No more indoor meetings—too risky. I'll be waiting on one of those benches next to the fountain in Park Place."

"Thinking of Craig?"

Vernon nodded. "There's always the odd chance that he has more of those gadgets of his planted around the place."

"When are we going to do something about him?"

"Thursday morning," Vernon said. "Right after the job and just before we leave." He leaned forward and his voice was cold. "And you can forget about the *we* part right now. I settle with Craig personally—understand?"

It was cold in the mortuary and when Jack Brady lifted the sheet to reveal Billy Stratton's face it was pale and bloodless.

"But there isn't a mark on him," Grant said.

"I wouldn't look any lower if I were you," Miller told him.

"What a way to go. You're satisfied with the circumstances?"

"Oh, yes, the driver of that bus didn't stand a chance. It was raining heavily at the time and Stratton simply plunged across the road, head-down. He'd been drinking, by the way."

"Much?"

"Five or six whiskies according to the blood sample."

Grant nodded to Brady, who replaced the sheet. "Who did the formal identification?"

"Ben Carver—reluctantly, I might add."

Brady chuckled. "I had to twist his arm a little. He wasn't too pleased."

"Oh, well, I'm not going to weep crocodile tears over the likes of Billy Stratton," Grant said. "We're well rid of him." He shivered. "I don't know why, but this place always makes me thirsty. They must be open by now. Let's go and have one."

The saloon bar of the George had just opened and they had the place to themselves. They stood at the bar and Grant ordered brandies all round.

"What about these two villains who had a go at

Craig last night?" he asked Miller. "Have you got anywhere with them?"

"Hurst and Blakely?" Miller shook his head. "A couple of real hard knocks. We've had a sheet on each of them from C.R.O. a yard long."

"Which means they were specially imported," Brady said.

Grant nodded. "I don't like the sound of that at all." He swallowed some of his brandy and gazed down into the glass reflectively. "You know I'm beginning to think I may have been wrong about this whole thing, Nick. It's just that it seemed such an incredible idea."

"Duncan Craig's a pretty incredible person," Miller said. "I tried to make that clear at the very beginning."

"Have you seen him since last night?"

Miller shook his head. "I tried this morning, but he wasn't available. Gone to Manchester on business I was told. Of course he'll have to come in to swear a formal complaint."

"When he does, let me know. I think I'd better have a word with him myself."

"You'll be wasting your time, sir," Miller said. "He'll insist that the whole thing was quite simply a common assault and we can't prove otherwise."

"But Hurst and Blakely won't get more than six months apiece for that."

"Exactly."

Grant frowned. "There's no chance at all that they might crack and admit who hired them?"

"If I know Max Vernon, they won't even know his name," Miller said.

Grant sighed and emptied his glass. "All in a day's work I suppose. Let's have another one."

"On me," Miller said.

"Oh no you don't," a cheerful voice interrupted. "My round. The same again, Maggie, and make them big ones."

Chuck Lazer grinned hugely as he climbed onto a stool next to Brady.

"What's all this?" Miller demanded. "Last time I saw you, you were on your knees."

"With the world falling in on me, but not now, boy. Not with the pressure off."

"What are you talking about?"

"Max Vernon." Lazer shrugged. "I mean he's on the run, isn't he? Everyone knows his betting shops have taken a hammering since the Flamingo closed and now last night's little affair."

"And what little affair would that be?" Brady put in.

"Come off it," Chuck said. "You know what I'm talking about. That place he was running up the York Road. The cut liquor racket." He chuckled. "He was making a packet there, too."

"You mean Max Vernon was behind that place?"

"Sure—everyone knows that." Lazer looked surprised. "Didn't you?"

Miller looked at Grant. "See what I mean, sir?"

Grant sighed. "All right. So I was wrong, but just try proving it, that's all. Just try proving it."

Park Place was a green oasis on the fringe of the city centre surrounded by old Victorian terrace houses already scheduled for demolition to make way for an inner Ring Road.

It was much favoured by office workers during their lunch-break, but at three-thirty when Max Vernon arrived it was quite deserted except for the cars parked round the edges and the small, greying man in the camel-hair coat who sat on a bench near the fountain.

He was reading a newspaper and didn't even bother

to look up when Vernon sat beside him. "I hope you aren't wasting my time?"

"Did I ever, Joe?"

"What about that Cable Diamonds job? I got nicked—five hard years while you sat laughing your head off in some fancy club or other."

"Luck of the draw."

"You never get involved personally, do you, Vernon? You never dirty your hands."

"Two hundred to two hundred and ten thousand quid, Joe. Are you in or out?"

Morgan's jaw dropped. "Two hundred grand? You must be joking."

"I never joke. You should know that by now."

"What's in it for me?"

"Half—you provide your own team and pay them out of your cut."

"And what in the hell do you do?"

"I've done my share." Vernon patted his briefcase. "It's all here, Joe. Everything you could possibly need and it'll go like clockwork—you know me. I never miss a trick."

"Not where you're concerned you don't." Morgan shook his head. "I don't know. Fifty per cent. That's a big slice to one man."

"You'll only need three men in the team. Give them ten thousand each—contract it beforehand. That still leaves you with seventy—maybe more." Morgan sat there, a frown on his face, and Vernon shrugged. "Please yourself. I'll get somebody else."

He started to his feet and Morgan pulled him back. "All right—no need to get shirty. I'm in."

"On my terms?"

"Whatever you say. When do we make the touch?"

"Wednesday night."

"You must be joking. That only gives us two days."

"No, it's got to be then—you'll see why in a moment. There's an express to London in an hour. You'll catch it easily. That'll give you plenty of time to recruit your team, gather your gear together and be back here by tomorrow night."

"What will I need?"

"That depends. You'll do the vault yourself?"

"Naturally. What is it?"

"Bodine-Martin 53—the latest model. Burglar proof naturally."

"They always are." Morgan chuckled. "A snip."

"What will you use—nitro?"

"Not on your life." Morgan shook his head.

"There's some new stuff the Army's been experimenting with going the rounds. Handles like nitro, but three times as powerful. It'll open that vault up like a sardine can."

"How long will you need?"

"On the vault itself?" He shrugged. "I'll have to cut a hole into the lock. Let's say forty-five minutes."

"And twenty to get you inside." Vernon nodded. "Just over an hour. Let's say an hour and a half from going in to coming out."

"Sounds too good to be true."

"You'll need a good wheelman to stand by with the car."

"Frankie Harris is available. He's just out of the Ville. Could do with some gelt."

"What about a labourer?"

"That's settled to start with—Johnny Martin. He knows how I like things done."

"And a good heavy and I don't mean some punch-drunk old has-been. You'll need someone who can really handle himself, just in case of trouble, though I don't think he'll even have to flex his muscles.

"I know just the man," Morgan said. "Jack Fallon. He used to run with Bart Keegan and the Poplar boys, but they had a row."

Vernon nodded approvingly. "That's a good choice. I remember Fallon. He's got brains, too."

"Okay—now that's settled let's get down to brass tacks. What's the pitch?"

"Chatsworth Iron & Steel down by the river. Only five minutes from where we are now as a matter of fact. Nine thousand workers and the management are still daft enough to pay them in cash. It takes the staff two days to make the wages up, which means there's never less than two hundred thousand, sometimes as much as two hundred and twenty in the vault Wednesday and Thursday, depending on earnings of course."

"Isn't there a night shift?"

"Only for the workers. The admin. side closes down at five-thirty on the dot. It's housed in a brand-new ten-storey office block between the factory and the river and they've installed just about every kind of alarm known to man."

"Bound to with loot like that lying around. How do we get in?"

"About a hundred yards from the factory there's a side street called Brag Alley. I've marked it on the map I'm giving you. Lift the manhole at the far end and you'll find yourself in a tunnel about three feet in diameter that carries the Electricity Board main cables. You'll know when you've reached Chatsworth Steel because they've been obliging enough to paint it on the wall. There's a single-course brick wall between you and the cellars of the office block. If it takes you longer than ten minutes to get through that I'll eat my hat."

"What about the alarm system?"

"I'm coming to that. When you get into the cellar you'll find a battery of fuse boxes on the far wall and they're all numbered. I've numbered the ones you'll have to switch off in your instructions, but the most important thing to remember is to cut the green cable you'll find running along the skirting board. It looks innocent enough, but it controls an alarm feeder system in case the others fail."

"Are the vaults on the same level?"

"That's right—at the far end of the corridor."

"What about night guards?"

"They only have one." Morgan raised his eyebrows incredulously and Vernon grinned. "I told you they'd installed every gadget known to man. The whole place is rigged for closed-circuit television, which is operated by one man from a control room off the main entrance hall. The moment you leave that cellar and walk down the passage you'll be giving a command performance. All he does is lift the 'phone and the coppers are all over you before you know it."

"Okay," Morgan said. "The suspense is killing me. How do we sort that one out?"

"They run a three-shift system and our man takes over at eight. He always stops in at a little café near the main gates for sandwiches and a flask of coffee. On Wednesday night he'll get more than he bargained for."

"Something in his coffee?"

Vernon grinned. "Simple when you know how."

Morgan looked dubious. "What if he hasn't had a drink by the time we arrive. We'd be in dead lumber."

"I've thought of that. You won't break in till midnight. That gives him four hours. If he hasn't had a drink by then, he never will."

There was a long silence as Morgan sat staring into the distance, a slight frown on his face. After a while he sighed and shook his head.

"I've got to give it to you, Max. It's good—it's bloody good."

"See you tomorrow night then," Vernon said calmly and passed him the briefcase. "Everything you need is in there. Your train leaves at five o'clock. You've got twenty minutes."

He watched Morgan disappear into the side street in the far corner of the square and nodded. So far, so good. The sun burst through the clouds, touching the fine spray of the fountain with colour and he smiled. There were times when life could really be very satisfying. He lit a cigarette, got to his feet and strolled away.

Duncan Craig watched him leave from the rear window of the old Commer van which was parked on the far side of the square. He, too, was smiling, but for a completely different reason. He turned and patted the chromium barrel of the directional microphone mounted on its tripod and started to dismantle it.

CHAPTER 12

It was raining hard when the van turned into Brag Alley and braked to a halt, the light from the headlamps picking out the faded lettering of the sign on the wooden doors that blocked the far end. *Gower & Co—Monumental Masons.*

"This is it," Morgan said. "Right—let's have you, Jack."

Fallon, a large, heavily built Irishman, jumped out, a pair of two-foot cutters in his hands that sliced through the padlock that secured the gates like a knife through butter. The gates swung open and Harris, the wheelman, took the van into the yard and cut the engine.

Fallon was already levering up the manhole in the alley and Morgan and Martin unloaded the van quickly and joined him. He dropped into the tunnel and they passed down the heavy cylinders for the oxy-acetyline cutter and the other equipment and followed him.

Harris dropped to one knee and Morgan whispered "Replace the manhole, shut yourself into the yard and sit tight. An hour and a quarter at the most."

The manhole clanged into place above his head as he dropped down to join the others. He switched on the powerful battery lantern he carried and its beam cut into the darkness. In spite of the thick cables, there was room to crawl and he moved off without a word, Fallon and Martin following, each dragging a canvas hold-all containing the equipment.

It was bitterly cold, the insulating jackets of the heavy cables damp with condensation, and at one point there was a sudden whispering like dead leaves rustling through a forest in the evening and a pair of eyes gleamed through the darkness.

"Jesus Christ, rats," Jack Fallon said. "I can't stand them."

"At these prices you can afford to," Morgan said and paused as his torch picked out the name Chatsworth Steel painted in white letters on the wall. "Here we are."

"Not much room to swing," Martin commented.

"Never mind that. Get the bloody gear out and let's have a go."

Martin was a small, undersized man with prematurely white hair, but his arms and shoulders were over-developed from a spell of working in the rock quarry at Dartmoor and he lay on his side and swung vigorously with a seven-pound hammer at the cold chisel which Fallon held in position.

When the wall gave, it was not one, but a dozen bricks which collapsed suddenly into the cellar on the other side. Martin grinned, his teeth gleaming in the light of the lamp.

"There's present-day British workmanship for you. I don't know what the country's coming to."

Morgan shone his lantern into the darkness on the other side and picked out the control panel at once. "Come on, let's get in there," he said. "We're right on time. Let's keep it that way."

It was the work of a couple of minutes to enlarge

the hole sufficiently to allow him to pass through and he left the others to manage the equipment and made straight for the control panel.

There were thirty-seven boxes on the board, each one numbered, and he had to pull the switch on nine of them. He had memorised the numbers, but checked them from the list Vernon had given him just to make sure.

"Everything okay?" Martin said at his shoulder.

"Couldn't be sweeter." Morgan dropped to one knee, located the green cable running along the edge of the skirting board and severed it neatly with a pair of pocket cutters. "That's it unless Vernon's made a mistake somewhere, which I doubt."

When he opened the door, the outside corridor was brilliantly lit by neon light. "What in the hell is the idea of that?" Martin demanded.

"For the television cameras, you fool. They wouldn't see much in the dark, would they?" Morgan led the way out into the corridor and grinned tightly. "Keep your fingers crossed. If that bloke upstairs is still awake, he's seen us already."

"I can't see any cameras," Martin said in bewilderment.

"No, but they can see you." Morgan paused at

the foot of the service stairs. "You stay here. Jack and I will go and take a look."

He went up the stairs quickly. The door at the top had a Yale lock and therefore opened from the inside with no difficulty.

The hall was tiled in black and white and brilliantly illuminated, its great glass doors protected by a bronze security grill. Morgan knew exactly where he was making for. He crossed the hall quickly, found the third door on the right with *Control Room* painted on it in black letters and turned the handle gently.

The guard had obviously tumbled from the black leather swivel chair in front of the control panel and sprawled on his face. The thermos flask stood open on a small table at one side and Morgan poured a little into the empty cup and tested it.

"Cold—he's been out for ages."

"Would you look at this now?" Fallon said in wonder.

There were at least thirty separate screens on the control panel. Not only was every entrance to the building covered, but cameras had obviously been positioned at strategic sites in all the main corridors.

"There's Johnny," Fallon said, pointing.

They could see Martin clearly as he stood in the basement corridor, the two canvas hold-alls at his feet.

"Looks nervous, doesn't he?" Morgan said and leaned forward. "There's the entrance to the strong-room and that's a picture of the vault door. Look, they've even got a shot of the interior. Would you credit it."

"It's fantastic," Fallon said. "You can see everything from up here."

Morgan nodded. "Come to think of it, it might be a good idea if you stayed up here, Jack. You've got every entrance to the building covered. If anyone did turn up, you'd know in a flash. Johnny and I can manage below."

"And how will I know when to join you?" Fallon said.

"You'll see on the screen, won't you?"

Fallon grinned delightedly. "And so I will. Off you go then, Joe, and God bless the good work."

Morgan went down the service stairs quickly and rejoined Martin. "Let's get moving," he said and picked up one of the canvas hold-alls.

The entrance to the strongroom was at the end of the passage, a steel door with a double padlock that took him exactly three minutes to pick.

He crossed the room quickly and examined the face of the vault door, testing the handles. Behind him, Martin had already got the first cylinder out of his hold-all. He screwed home one end of the flexible hose that connected it to the blow torch and ignited the flame.

Morgan pulled on a pair of protective goggles and held out his hand. "Okay, let's get to work," he said.

A few moments later he was cutting into the steel face of the vault, six inches to the right of the locking mechanism, with the precision of an expert.

For something like forty-five minutes, Jack Fallon had a seat at the show that couldn't have been bettered if he'd been sitting in the front circle at his local cinema. He leaned back in the swivel chair, smoking one cigarette after the other, intent on the drama that was being enacted below.

He was at Morgan's side when he finished cutting the hole and waited, biting his fingernails, while the explosive was gently poured inside the lock, sealed with a plastic compound and fused.

He heard no noise, but the visual effect of the explosion was dramatic enough. The door seemed to tremble, then a portion of it around the lock seemed to disintegrate before his eyes and smoke rose in a cloud.

He saw Morgan and Martin rush forward, heaving on the door together, swinging it open, and switched his gaze to the next screen in time to see them enter the interior of the vault itself.

He jumped to his feet, excitement racing through him, started to turn away and paused, a cold chill spreading through his body.

He was looking at another screen—the one that gave a view of the passageway linking the cellar by which they had entered the building with the strong-room. A man was moving along the passage cautiously, tall and dark in sweater and pants, gloves on his hands and a nylon stocking pulled over his face.

Fallon cursed savagely, turned and ran to the door, knocking over the chair in his haste.

. . .

Beyond the van a monumental cross reared into the night and here and there, marble tombstones gleamed palely. The mason's yard was dark and lonely, a place of shadows that was too much like a cemetery for comfort and Frankie Harris huddled into the driver's seat miserably, hands thrust deep into the pockets of his overcoat.

He was getting old, that was the trouble—too old for this sort of action by night. He seemed to have been waiting there for hours and yet it was no more than forty-five minutes since his three companions had entered the manhole.

His feet were so cold that he could no longer feel them and after a while he opened the door and stepped into the rain. He walked up and down for a minute or two, stamping his feet to restore the circulation, and then paused to light a cigarette, his hands cupped around the flaring match.

He gave a sudden, terrible start as the light picked a face out of the night—a dark, formless face lacking eyes and mouth that could belong to nothing human.

He staggered back in horror, the match dropping from his nerveless fingers, and his throat was seized in a grip of iron.

"Frank Harris?" The thing had a voice. "You're just out of the Ville, aren't you?"

The pressure was released and Harris nodded violently. "That's right."

"How long?"

"Ten days."

"You bloody fool." Suddenly he found himself being jerked round and propelled towards the gate. "Now start running," the voice said harshly, "and don't stop. Anything that happens to you after this, you deserve."

Harris ran along the alley as he hadn't run since he was a boy and when he reached the end, paused, leaning against the wall.

"Christ Jesus," he sobbed. "Oh, Christ Jesus."

After a while he pulled himself together, turned into the main road and started walking briskly in the direction of the Central Station.

Duncan Craig moved rapidly along the tunnel towards the patch of light that streamed in through the broken wall from the cellar. When he reached the opening he paused to examine his watch, wondering if he had timed things right and a sudden, muffled explosion reverberating throughout the basement told him that he had.

He dropped into the cellar and moved out into the passage, a strange and sinister figure in his dark clothing, a nylon stocking pulled down over his face.

A cloud of dust and smoke filtered out through the half open door of the strongroom at the far end of the passage and he moved towards it cautiously and peered inside.

The room was full of dust and smoke and beyond through the half open vault door, he was aware of a vague movement. He stepped back into the passageway and slammed the strongroom door shut, jerking down the handle, the locking bolts clanging into their sockets with a grim finality. Without the key he was unable to actually lock the door, but the important thing was that it would be impossible for it to be opened from the inside. He turned and moved back along the passage.

As he passed the entrance to the service stairs, Fallon jumped on him from five steps up, fourteen stone of bone and muscle driving Craig into the floor.

For the moment, he was winded and as he struggled for air, the Irishman's massive forearm wrapped itself around his throat. As the pressure increased, Craig rammed the point of his right elbow back hard, catching Fallon in the stomach just under the rib cage. Fallon gasped and again Craig drove his elbow home with all his force. As the Irishman's grip slackened, Craig twisted round and slammed him backwards with the heel of his hand.

Fallon rolled against the wall, the instinct derived from a hundred street fights bringing him to his feet in a reflex action, but Craig was already up and waiting for him. As Fallon moved in, Craig's right foot flicked out in a perfectly executed *karate* front kick that caught the Irishman in the stomach. He started to keel over, and Craig's knee lifted into his face like a battering ram, sending him into darkness.

Ruth Miller waved the last of her guests goodbye and closed the door. She looked at her watch and smothered a yawn. One o'clock. A good party and the clearing up could wait till morning. She started across the hall and the 'phone rang.

Nick Miller and his brother were having a final drink in front of the fire when she looked in. "It's for you, Nick. He wouldn't say who he was. I do hope you don't have to go out."

"On a night like this? Not on your life." He went out into the hall and picked up the 'phone.

"That you, Miller?"

"Yes, who is it?"

"Never mind that. Chatsworth Iron & Steel—they usually keep a couple of hundred thousand in their vault on a Wednesday night, don't they? You'd better get down there quick. They almost lost it." There was a hoarse chuckle. "Poor old Maxie. Talk about the best-laid schemes . . ."

But Miller had already cut him off and was dialling the best-known telephone number in England furiously.

The main C.I.D. office was a hive of industry when Grant entered at two a.m. and Miller got up from his desk and went to meet him.

"Well, this is a turn up for the book and no mistake," Grant said.

"You've had a look at Chatsworth's, sir?"

"Never seen anything like it. Any chance of a cup of tea?"

Miller nodded to a young D.C. who disappeared at once and they went into Grant's office.

"What about the guard?"

"I've just had a 'phone call from the man I sent

with him to the Infirmary. Apparently his coffee was laced with enough chloral hydrate to put him asleep for twelve hours so he still hasn't come round."

"Who have we got in the bag?"

"Joe Morgan for one."

"Have we, by George?" Grant's eyebrows went up. "We certainly don't need a scratch sheet on him. One of the best petermen in the game. Was Johnny Martin with him?"

Miller nodded. "That's right."

"I thought so—they usually work together. Who else?"

"We found a nasty-looking piece of work lying in the basement passageway. He'd taken quite a beating."

"Is he okay now?"

"Alive and kicking, but making things awkward for us. Jack Brady's running his fingerprints through C.R.O. now. We found their transport, by the way, parked in a monumental mason's yard in Brag Alley at the other end of the tunnel which they used to gain access. No sign of a wheelman."

"Maybe they didn't use one."

"Could be—I've put out a general call anyway, just in case."

The tea arrived and Grant drank some grate-
fully, warming his hands around the cup. "Fantastic,
Nick—that's the only word for it. This thing was
planned to the last inch, you realise that don't you?
They'd have been in London by morning. God knows
where after that."

"Except for an elusive someone who shut the
strongroom door on Morgan and Martin and left
this other bloke lying unconscious in the passageway."

"Your informer, presumably. And he mentioned
Vernon?"

"As far as I'm concerned he did. Vernon's the
only Maxie I know and planning a job like this
would be right up his street."

Grant emptied his cup and sighed. "I suppose
you think it's Craig?"

"I can't see who else it could be."

"No, I suppose not."

"Do I pull him in for questioning?"

"On what charge?" Grant spread his hands. "We'd
have to think up a brand-new one just for him."

"What about accessary before the fact? He knew
the caper was coming off—he should have passed on
the information to us."

"I can't imagine a judge giving him more than a stern wigging for that. Anyway, how could Craig have obtained such detailed information?"

"Simple," Miller said. "He's an electronics expert. Directional microphones, transistor transmitters the size of matchboxes, fountain pen receivers. You name it, he's got it."

"Nothing illegal in that considering the nature of his business." Grant shook his head. "Proof, Nick—real proof. That's what you need. You haven't got it and you never will have unless I miss my guess."

"All right," Miller said. "You win. What about Vernon? Do we bring him in?"

Grant hesitated. "No, let him stew for a while. He's always covered his tracks perfectly in the past so there's no reason to think things will be any easier for us this time. If we're going to get him, it must be through Morgan and his boys. Put two men on watch at his club and leave it at that for the moment."

Brady knocked on the door and entered, a sheaf of teletype flimsies in his hand. "I thought I'd get the facts on all of them while I was at it. Our awkward friend is a bloke called Jack Fallon—a real tearaway. He's even done time for manslaughter."

"He certainly met his match this time," Grant said.

Miller was reading the reports quickly and he suddenly frowned. "Cable Diamonds—that has a familiar sound."

"It should have," Brady said. "It was mentioned in that confidential file on Vernon that we got from C.R.O. in London. Another of the jobs he was supposed to be behind."

Miller grinned. "You're going to love this, sir," he said to Grant and passed one of the flimsies across. "Joe Morgan was nicked for that job after getting clean away. He did five years, but the diamonds were never recovered."

"He doesn't seem to be having much luck with Max Vernon, does he?" Brady said.

Grant nodded and got to his feet. "Let's go and remind him of that fact, shall we?"

CHAPTER 13

From one-thirty onwards Max Vernon knew in his heart that something had gone badly wrong. By two-fifteen he was sure of it. He poured himself a large brandy, went to his desk and flicked one of the switches on the intercom.

"Get in here, Ben."

The door opened a few moments later and Carver entered. "Yes, Mr. Vernon?"

"Something's up—they're way over time. Take the car and go for a drive past Chatsworth's. See if you can see any action."

Carver nodded obediently and left and Vernon lit a cigarette and moved across to the fire. He stared down into the flames, a frown on his face. What could have possibly gone wrong? It didn't make any kind of sense. The thing was foolproof.

The door swung open behind him and Carver came in looking pale and excited. "A couple of coppers out front, Mr. Vernon."

"Are you sure?"

"Certain—I can smell 'em a mile away. I'll show you."

Vernon followed him out into the corridor and Carver turned into the cloakroom and paused by the window. "I came in for my overcoat. Lucky I didn't turn on the light." He pointed across to the sycamore on the other side of the fence beyond the first street lamp. "There, in the shadows "

"Yes, I've got them."

"What do you think?"

"I think it stinks to high heaven," Vernon said, and the telephone started to ring in the other room.

He moved back quickly, Carver at his heels, and stood by the desk looking down at the 'phone.

"It's Morgan," Carver said. "It has to be. Who else would be ringing in at this time in the morning?"

"We'll see shall we? You take it on the extension." Vernon lifted the receiver. "Max Vernon here."

"That you, old man?" Craig's voice rang mockingly in his ear. "I'm afraid Joe Morgan and his boys won't be able to join you after all. They ran into a little trouble."

Vernon sank down in his chair. "I'll kill you for this, Craig."

"You've had it," Craig said cheerfully. "Joe Morgan and his boys are being squeezed dry at this very moment. How long do you think it will be before one of them spills his guts? You're on borrowed time, Vernon."

"As long as I've enough left for you that's all I ask," Vernon said.

"Sorry, old man. I've decided to take myself off into the country for a couple of days' shooting. Nothing like a change of pace. If you want me, you'll have to come looking."

He was still chuckling as Vernon slammed down the receiver. Carver replaced the extension 'phone, a bewildered look on his face. "But how could he have known?"

"How the hell do I know? Another of his damned gadgets probably."

"What do we do now?"

"Get out while the going's good—on foot the back

way. I've got an old Ford brake parked in a lock-up garage on the other side of the river. I always did believe in covering every eventuality."

"Where are we going, Mr. Vernon—Ireland?"

"You can if you like. I can manage a couple of hundred. That should see you through."

"What about you?"

Vernon unlocked a drawer in his desk and took out a Luger pistol. "I've got an account to settle."

"With Craig? You don't even know where he's going."

"I shouldn't imagine I'll have any difficulty in finding out."

Carver frowned in bewilderment. "I don't get it."

"A challenge, Benny. A challenge—something you wouldn't understand."

"You mean Craig wants you to follow him?"

Vernon opened the wall safe and took out a black cash box. "That's the general idea." He returned to his desk with the cash box and unlocked it. "This is what he's been aiming at from the beginning—him and me in a final showdown, but he's made a big mistake." When Vernon smiled he looked like the Devil incarnate. "I was a good man in the jungle,

Ben—the best there was. Craig's still got to find that out."

He opened the cash box, tossed two packets of fivers across and started to fill his pockets with the rest. "There's two hundred there and good luck to you."

Carver shook his head slowly and threw the money back. "We've been together a long time, Mr. Vernon. I'm not dropping out now."

Vernon stared at him incredulously. "Loyalty at this stage, Ben?" And then he laughed harshly and clapped him on the shoulder. "All right then. Let's see if we can't show the bastard a thing or two."

"But who turned you in, Morgan, that's what I can't understand?" Miller said.

It was just after four a.m. and the pale green walls of the Interrogation Room seemed to float out of the shadows, unreal and transitory as if they might disappear at any moment.

Joe Morgan sat at the plain wooden table under a strong central light that made him look old and sunken. Brady leaned against the wall near the window and a young constable stood stolidly in the corner.

"Nobody turned us in. The whole thing went sour, that's all."

"Then who closed the strongroom door on you and Martin?"

"I don't know—maybe it just slammed shut."

"All right, miracles sometimes happen. That still doesn't explain how we found Jack Fallon lying beaten and unconscious in the passageway."

Morgan didn't reply and Brady said helpfully, "Maybe Fallon just doesn't like you anymore. Maybe he decided to lock you and Martin in the strongroom just for kicks and took off. Unfortunately he tripped and fell in the passage, knocking himself unconscious."

Morgan turned away contemptuously. "You ought to see a psychiatrist."

"We'll provide you with one for free," Miller said. "You're going to need him badly, Morgan. You're going to sit for the next ten years staring at the wall, asking yourself the same question over and over again until it drives you out of your mind."

Morgan snapped, suddenly and completely. "But I don't know what went wrong. I don't know." He hammered on the table with a clenched fist. "Can't you get that through your thick skull?"

In the silence which followed Grant peered round the door, eyebrows raised. Miller shook his head, nodded to Brady and they joined the superintendent in the corridor.

"Anything?" Grant said.

Miller shook his head. "No more success than we've had with the others."

"He seems genuinely bewildered to me," Brady put in. "I get the impression he'd like to know what happened as much as anybody."

"Right," Grant said briskly. "This is where keeping them separate might have paid off. Put them together in cell 15 and let's see what happens."

When the constable pushed Joe Morgan into the cell, Martin was sitting despondently on a bench against the wall. Morgan frowned in bewilderment as the door closed behind him.

"What is this?"

Martin shrugged. "Search me."

"Maybe the place is wired for sound?"

Morgan looked the walls over carefully and behind

him, the door opened again and Jack Fallon was pushed into the cell. He looked a mess. His lips were swollen and gashed, several teeth missing and the front of his shirt was soaked in blood.

He staggered forward, a wild look in his eyes and grabbed Morgan by the lapels. "What happened for Christ's sake? Who was he?"

Morgan tore himself free with some difficulty. "Who was who?"

"The bloke who came in through the tunnel and locked you and Johnny in the strongroom."

"What are you talking about?" Morgan demanded.

"I'm trying to tell you. I saw him on the bloody television screen. Big bloke all in black with a stocking over his face. He locked you and Johnny in the strongroom and I jumped him from the stairs."

"You had a barney?"

"Not for long. Henry Cooper couldn't have hit me any harder than he did."

"Maybe it was Harris?" Martin said.

"Do me a favour." Fallon laughed harshly. "I could break him in two with one hand tied behind my back. It wouldn't make sense anyway. What would he stand to gain?"

"Then why haven't they put him in with the rest of us?"

"Search me."

Morgan turned away, his hands gripped tightly together. "Only one man knew we were pulling this caper," he said. "The man who organised it."

"Vernon?" Martin's eyes widened. "It don't make sense, Joe."

"I've just got one prayer," Morgan said. "That one day they put him in the same nick as me. That's all I ask."

In the next cell, Grant reached up to switch off the tannoy and nodded to Miller and Brady. "That'll do me. In we go."

They went out into the passage and the constable who was standing at the door of cell 15 unlocked it quickly and stood back.

"Did I hear somebody mention Max Vernon's name?" Grant said as he led the way in.

"Why don't you take a running jump at yourself," Morgan told him bitterly.

"Oh, to hell with it." Jack Fallon cursed savagely. "If you think I'm going to rot while that bastard goes free you can think again. If you don't tell him, I will."

"You don't have much luck with Vernon, do you?" Grant said to Morgan. "Remember that Cable Diamond affair? I suppose he saw you all right when you came out."

"Five hundred," Morgan said. "Five hundred quid for five bloody years in the nick." The anger came pouring out of him in an uncontrollable flood. "All right—Vernon's your man and much good it'll do you. We were supposed to be back at his place no later than one-thirty. If he's still there when you call then I'm Santa Claus."

It was almost five-thirty when Miller went into Grant's office. The superintendent was reading through the statements made by Morgan and his cronies and looked up sharply.

"Any luck?"

"Not a sign. Must have cleared out the back way on foot. I've put out a general call. We've alerted the County and the Regional Crime Squad as well."

"He'll probably try for the Irish boat at Liverpool." Grant said. "He won't get far."

"I'm not so sure, sir. What if he's still in town?"

"Why should he be?"

"There's always Craig. He has a score to settle there."

"I shouldn't think he'd be foolish enough to hang around while he still had time to get out."

"All the same, sir, I'd like your permission to give Craig a ring. I'd feel happier."

Grant leaned back in his chair and looked at him reflectively. "You like him, don't you?"

"I suppose the simple answer to that is yes—a hell of a lot."

Grant indicated the 'phone on his desk with a sweep of his hand. "Be my guest."

The 'phone rang for a long time at the other end before it was lifted and Harriet Craig said sleepily, "Yes, who is it?"

"Harriet—is that you? Nick Miller here."

"Nick?" There was a pause and he had a mental picture of her struggling up onto one elbow, a bewildered frown on her face. "Nick, what time is it?"

"Twenty to six. I was hoping to speak to your father."

"I'm afraid he's gone away for a few days." Suddenly, her voice changed and she came wide awake. "What is it, Nick? Is something wrong?"

There was genuine alarm in her voice and he hastened to reassure her. "Everything's all right, I promise you. Are you on your own?"

"No, Jenny's here."

"Tell you what. How would you like to give me breakfast? I'll tell you all about it then."

"That's fine by me. What time?"

"Seven-thirty too early?"

"Not at all. If you think I could go to sleep again after this you're mistaken."

Miller replaced the receiver and turned to Grant. "She's on her own—her father's out of town. Mind if I put a car on watch up there? Just in case."

"Just in case?" Grant said and smiled. "Young love—it's marvellous. Go on—get out of here."

It was raining heavily when Miller drove up to the house and the patrol car was parked by the entrance to the drive. He got out of the Cooper and walked across and the driver wound down his window.

"Anything?" Miller asked.

"Not a thing, sarge. Some bird came out of the door about five minutes ago and took a walk in the garden, that's all. She must be nuts in this weather."

"Okay," Miller said. "I'll take over. You can shove off now."

The patrol car moved away and he got back into the Cooper and drove up to the house. As he got out, a voice hailed him and he turned to find Harriet crossing the lawn. She was wearing an old trenchcoat of her father's and a scarf was bound around her head peasant-fashion.

"I saw the police car at the gate when I came downstairs," she said, her face grave. "What is it, Nick?"

"Maybe we'd better go inside."

"No, I'd rather not. Jenny's in the kitchen . . ."

"And she doesn't know what you and your father have been up to, is that it?"

She turned away, an angry flush staining her cheeks, and he pulled her round to face him. "You said your father had gone away for a few days. Is that the truth?"

"Of course it is."

"And you didn't know what he was up to last night?"

She shook her head, her eyes anxious. "Please, Nick—I don't know what you're talking about."

He looked at her searchingly for a moment and then nodded. "All right—I believe you."

He sketched in the events of the night briefly and when he finished, she looked pale and drawn. "I can't believe it."

"But you knew about the other things."

She gazed up at him searchingly. "Are you here as a friend, Nick, or as a policeman?"

"As a friend, damn you." He took her hands and held them fast. "You must believe that."

She nodded. "Yes, I knew about the other things. It seemed wrong somehow that Max Vernon should get away with what he did." She looked up at him fiercely. "I'm not sorry."

"You will be if he gets his hands on your father."

"You think that's possible?"

"Not really, he's too many other problems facing him at the moment, but you never can tell what a man like Vernon might pull. We'd better give your father a ring just in case."

"But there isn't a 'phone," she said. "He's staying in our houseboat on the river at Grimsdyke."

"In the marshes?"

"That's right, he goes for the shooting."

"That's about twenty miles, isn't it?"

"Eighteen on the clock."

"Good—we'll drive down and see him. It's early

yet and the roads will be quiet. Shouldn't take more than half an hour."

She nodded briefly. "I'd better tell Jenny. I'll only be a moment."

She turned and ran across the lawn to the terrace and Miller walked back to the car.

It was no more than ten minutes after they had left when the 'phone rang and Jenny answered it on the kitchen extension.

"Colonel Craig's residence."

The voice was smooth and charming. "Good morning—my name's Fullerton. Gregory Fullerton. I'm a colleague of Colonel Craig's. He told me he was going away for a few days and gave me his address so that I could get in touch with him if anything came up. Damned stupid of me, but I've mislaid it."

"It's the houseboat you'll be wanting, sir," Jenny said. "That's on the river at Grimsdyke in the marshes about a mile south of Culler's Bend."

"So kind of you."

"Not at all." She replaced the receiver and went back to her work.

When Max Vernon emerged from the telephone box at the end of the small country lane he was grinning wolfishly. He opened the door of the brake and climbed into the passenger seat next to Carver.

"Right, Benny boy, we're in business," he said. "Let's have a look at that map."

CHAPTER 14

The marsh at Grimsdyke on the river estuary was a wild lonely place of sea-creeks and mud flats and great pale barriers of reeds higher than a man's head. Since the beginning of time men had come here for one purpose or another—Roman, Saxon, Dane, Norman, but in the twentieth century it was a place of ghosts, an alien world inhabited mainly by the birds, curlew and redshank and the brent geese coming south from Siberia to winter on the flats.

Miller turned the Cooper off the main road at Culler's Bend and followed a track no wider than a farm cart that was little more than a raised causeway of grass. On either side, miles of rough marsh grass and reeds marched into the heavy rain and a thin sea mist was drifting in before the wind.

Harriet lowered the window and took a deep breath of the salt-laden air. "Marvellous—I love coming here. It's like nowhere else on earth—a different world."

"I must say I'm impressed," he said. "I've never been here before."

"Lost in a marsh punt in a sea mist it can be terrifying," she said. "In some places there are quicksands and mud-holes deep enough to swallow a cart."

The closer they got to the estuary, the more the mist closed in on them until visibility was reduced to no more than twenty yards. Finally the track emerged into a wide clearing of rough grass surrounded by thorn trees. Craig's Jaguar was parked under one of them and Miller braked to a halt.

"We have to walk from here," Harriet said. "It isn't very far."

They followed a narrow path through the reeds. Wildfowl lifted out of the mist in alarm and somewhere a curlew called eerily. The marsh was stirring now, water swirling through it with an angry sucking noise, gurgling in crab holes, baring shining expanses of black mud.

"If we don't hurry we might miss him," Harriet said. "The tide's on the ebb. The best time for duck."

She half-ran along the track and Miller followed her and suddenly, the wind was cold on his face and she called through the rain, waving her hand.

The mist had cleared a little so that one could see the river, the houseboat moored to the bank forty or fifty yards away. Duncan Craig was about to step into a flat-bottomed marsh punt and straightened, looking towards them.

He was wearing an old paratrooper's beret and combat jacket and carried a shotgun under one arm. He stood there staring at them, one hand shielding his eyes from the rain and then ran forward suddenly.

His face was white and set when he grabbed Harriet by the arm, the first time Miller had known him to show real emotion. "What the hell are you doing here?"

Harriet was bewildered by the anger in his voice. "What is it, Daddy? What's wrong?"

"We tried to arrest Max Vernon early this morning, but he gave us the slip," Miller told him.

"I thought you ought to know he was on the loose."

Craig gave Harriet a quick push forward. "Get her out of here, Miller! Get her out now before it's too late!"

Harriet swung round, her face white, and Miller said softly, "My God, you're actually expecting him, aren't you? You've arranged the whole damned thing?"

"Every step of the way." Craig patted the shotgun. "Vernon shall have his chance—all part of the game."

"It isn't a game any longer, you bloody fool," Miller said. "Can't you get that through your head? If Max Vernon comes looking for you he'll have only one thought on his mind."

"Which suits me just fine." Suddenly there was iron in his voice. "No more arguments. Just get Harriet out of here."

Miller shrugged and said evenly, "All right, if that's the way you want it. I might point out that the first thing I shall do is contact the County Police."

"Good luck to you. There's a village bobby at Culler's Bend two miles up the road—Jack Berkley. He's fifty years of age and it takes him all his time to get on his bicycle."

"They do have such things as patrol cars."

"Fair enough—it'll be interesting to see just how efficient they are."

"He isn't worth it, Craig," Miller said desperately. "He isn't worth what it would do to you."

"He murdered my daughter," Craig said calmly. "He wasn't even fit to tie her shoes, but I'm still giving him his chance, Nick. God help me, but I can't play the game any other way."

"Which means only one thing in the final analysis. That you won't be able to kill him," Miller said. "Can't you see that? It's the essential difference between you and Vernon."

Craig didn't reply and Harriet simply stood there, white and terrified. Miller sighed and took her arm. "All right. Let's get going."

When they reached the clearing, he helped Harriet into the passenger seat of the Cooper, climbed behind the wheel quickly and started the engine. He slid back the window and leaned out.

"For the last time, Duncan—please."

Craig smiled strangely and leaned down. "Thanks, Nick—for everything. Now get her out of it, there's a good chap."

Miller moved into gear and took the Cooper back along the track and beside him Harriet started to sob bitterly.

"Oh, Nick, I'm so afraid," she said. "He isn't like Vernon—not when it comes down to it. He's going to die. I know he is."

"Not if I can help it." Miller said and braked violently as a Ford station wagon appeared from the mist.

The two cars were not more than twenty feet apart. For one horrified moment they stared at Max Vernon and Carver and then Miller slammed the stick into reverse and took the Cooper back along the track.

Vernon jumped out of the Ford, the Luger in his hand, and fired twice, his second shot punching a hole in the Cooper's windscreen. It slewed wildly and went half over the edge of the track.

As Miller got the door open Duncan Craig appeared on the run. He dropped to one knee and fired once in the direction of the Ford.

"You two all right?"

Harriet nodded shakily. "I think so."

"Get her down into the reeds," he told Miller

briskly. "I'll lead them off. As soon as they pass, get her out of here."

He scrambled to his feet before Miller could argue and ran through the mist towards the Ford.

Vernon waited, the Luger ready, and Carver crouched on the other side of the Ford, a Smith & Wesson revolver in his hand.

"Do you think it was Craig who fired that shot, Mr. Vernon?"

Craig answered for himself, his voice drifting mockingly out of the mist. "So you got here, Vernon? All right, then. Let's see how good you really are."

For a brief moment he appeared from the mist and turned and ran and Vernon went after him, cold with excitement.

They reached the Cooper half-blocking the track and Craig called, "This way, Vernon! This way!"

As they disappeared into the mist, Miller emerged from the reeds pulling Harriet behind him. They ran back along the track and paused beside the Ford. The key was missing from the dashboard, but he reached underneath, wrenched out the ignition wires and looped them together quickly. A moment later the engine roared into life.

He turned to Harriet. "Can you get this thing out of here?"

"I think so."

"Good—I noticed a telephone box about a mile up the road on the way in. Ring through to Grant—he'll know what to do. The County boys would probably wonder what in the hell you were talking about."

"What about you?"

"You don't think I'm going to let him cut his own throat at this stage do you?" He shoved her into the car. "Go on—get out of it!"

As the Ford reversed away, a pistol shot echoed across the marshes that was answered by the blast of a shotgun. Miller turned and ran along the track in the direction of the sound.

Duncan Craig turned off the path to the left, ran across an expanse of coarse marsh grass into the shelter of the mist and doubled back on his tracks. He paused and listened intently. The only sound was the lapping of water and further along, geese lifted into the sky, voicing their annoyance at being disturbed.

By all the rules he should now be behind Vernon and Carver and he moved out of the shelter of the mist and approached the path cautiously. Somewhere to the right, there was the sound of running footsteps and as he crouched, shotgun ready, Nick Miller ran out of the mist.

"Over here!" Craig called softly and Miller paused on the edge of the raised path and looked down at him, chest heaving.

"Thank God—I didn't think it would be this easy."

There was a sudden cold laugh and Max Vernon scrambled onto the path from the other side about twenty yards to the left. "It never is," he called harshly and his hand swung up.

The bullet caught Miller in the upper arm, knocking him back off the path into the soft earth as Craig fired his shotgun in reply. Max Vernon had already slipped back into cover and Craig reached down and dragged Miller to his feet.

"Can you still run?"

Miller nodded, his face white with shock. "I think so."

"Then let's get out of here."

They stumbled across the rough ground into the mist, two more bullets chasing them on their way, and suddenly the water was knee-deep and the reeds lifted to meet them.

Another bullet echoed wildly through the mist and Miller crouched instinctively, stumbling to one knee. Craig pulled him to his feet and they moved on through a thick glutinous slime covered by water, which in places was thigh deep.

Miller was conscious of the pain in his arm as the first shock wore off, of the coldness of the water as it ate into his flesh like acid, and struggled for breath.

Suddenly Craig disappeared with a startled cry, the water closing over his head. Miller lurched forward, reaching out, and followed him in. It was a terrible sensation as the filthy, stinking water forced its way into his mouth and nostrils. His feet could find no bottom as he struggled frantically and then an iron hand had him by the collar. A moment later, he was on his hands and knees amongst the reeds and breathing again.

Craig crouched beside him. He had lost his red beret and his face was streaked with black mud and slime. "All right?"

Miller coughed and brought up a little marsh water.

"What about you?"

"Lost the shotgun, I'm afraid. If you think you can keep on the move, we've a chance of circling round to the houseboat. There are a couple of sporting rifles and an extra shotgun there."

Miller nodded, getting to his feet, and they moved forward again. A couple of minutes later the reeds started to thin and a dyke lifted out of the mist. They scrambled up out of the water and Craig started to run at a jogtrot, Miller stumbling after him.

The pain in his arm was much worse now and there was a stitch in his side. He stumbled into a thorn tree at the top of a grassy knoll above a small, scum-covered pool and managed to cry out.

"No use, Duncan. I can't go on."

Craig didn't even attempt to argue. "Get out of sight and wait," he said crisply. "I'll be back in ten minutes."

There was a clump of bushes just below the path and Miller rolled underneath. He pillowed his cheek against the wet earth, struggling for breath, and was suddenly aware of footsteps approaching from the direction in which they had come. A moment later, Ben Carver came into view.

He paused, his feet no more than a yard away from Miller's head, the Smith & Wesson held in his left hand, and Miller didn't hesitate. He grabbed for the ankles with all his force. Carver fell on top of him, the Smith & Wesson flying out of his hand into the pool below.

Miller cried out in agony as the pain in his arm seemed to spread throughout his entire body and he reached for Carver's throat with his right hand. Together, they burst out of the bushes and rolled down the slope.

For the briefest of moments Miller was on top as they reached the bottom and he used it well. His right hand rose and fell, the edge catching Carver full across the throat. He screamed and turned over, tearing at his collar.

Miller tried to get to his feet and Max Vernon said, "Hold it right there—where's Craig?"

He was standing half-way down the slope, the Luger ready, his face pale. "Right here, Vernon!" Craig called.

He came down the slope like a rugby forward, head down, catching Vernon round the waist. The Luger exploded once and then they were locked together and falling backwards.

The waters of the pool closed over them and they rose separately. Vernon seemed bewildered, his face black with mud and Craig surged forward and hit him again and again, solid, heavy punches that drove him into the centre of the pool.

Vernon lost his balance and went under the surface. As he got to his feet, he screamed suddenly. "My legs—I can't move my legs! I'm sinking!"

Craig floundered back towards the edge of the pool, the mud releasing him reluctantly with great sucking noises. When he reached firm ground he turned, a slightly dazed expression on his face and wiped the back of a hand wearily across his eyes.

Vernon was going fast, the quagmire under the surface of the water drawing him down. "For God's sake, help me, Craig! Help me!"

Miller pushed himself to his feet and staggered forward clutching his arm, blood oozing between his fingers. Vernon was already chest-deep and he went to pieces completely, babbling hysterically, arms thrashing the water.

Miller started forward and Craig pulled him back. "And I thought it was going to be so easy," he said bitterly.

He unzipped his combat jacket, taking it off as he

waded into the pool. He held it by the end of one sleeve and reached out to Vernon.

"Hold on tight if you want to live."

Vernon grabbed for the other sleeve with both hands like a drowning man and Craig started backwards. He was already beginning to sink himself and for a moment, nothing seemed to be happening. Miller moved to help him, extending his one good arm, and Craig grabbed at his hand. A moment later, Vernon came out of the slime with a rush.

He crawled from the water and lay face down at the side of the pool, his whole body racked by sobbing. Miller and Craig moved back to the bottom of the slope and slumped down.

"So you were right and I was wrong?" Craig sighed wearily. "I should have known I couldn't go through with it."

"All part of the service," Miller said.

Craig turned with a wry grin. "It's been fun, hasn't it? We must do it again sometime."

As they started to laugh, a police whistle sounded somewhere in the distance and scores of brent geese rose in a protesting cloud and flew out to sea.

If you enjoyed *BROUGHT IN DEAD*,
you won't want to miss
HELL IS ALWAYS TODAY,
the latest thrilling novel from Jack Higgins.

Here's a brief excerpt . . .

Look for . . .

Hell Is Always Today

In bookstores May 2005!

Prologue

The police car turned the end of the street and pulled into the kerb beside the lamp. The driver kept the motor running, and grinned at his passenger.

"Rather you than me on a night like this, but I was forgetting. You love your work, don't you?"

Police Constable Henry Joseph Dwyer's reply was unprintable and he stood at the edge of the pavement, a strangely melancholy figure in the helmet and cape, listening to the sound of the car fade into the night. Rain fell steadily, drifting down through the yellow glow of the street lamp in a silver spray, and he turned morosely and walked towards the end of the street.

It was just after ten and the night stretched before

him, cold and damp. The city was lonely and for special reasons at that time, rather frightening even for an old hand like Joe Dwyer. Still, no point in worrying about that. Another ten months and he'd be out of it, but his hand still moved inside his cape to touch the small two-way radio in his breast pocket, the lifeline that could bring help when needed within a matter of minutes.

He paused on the corner and looked across the square towards the oasis of light that was the coffee stall on the other side. No harm in starting off with something warm inside him and he needed some cigarettes.

There was only one customer, a large, heavily built man in an old trenchcoat and rain hat who was talking to Sam Harkness, the owner. As Dwyer approached, the man turned, calling goodnight over his shoulder and plunged into the rain head down so that he and the policeman collided.

"Steady on there," Dwyer began and then recognised him. "Oh, it's you, Mr. Faulkner. Nasty night, sir."

Faulkner grinned. "You can say that again. I only came out for some cigarettes. Hope they're paying you double time tonight."

"That'll be the day, sir."

Faulkner walked away and Dwyer approached the stall. "He's in a hurry, isn't he?"

Harkness filled a mug with tea from the urn, spooned sugar into it and pushed it across. "Wouldn't you be if you was on your way home to a warm bed on a night like this? Probably got some young bird lying there in her underwear waiting for him. They're all the same these artists."

Dwyer grinned. "You're only jealous. Let's have twenty of the usual. Must have something to get me through the night. How's business?"

Harkness passed the cigarettes across and changed the ten-shilling note that Dwyer gave him. "Lucky if I make petrol money."

"I'm not surprised. You won't get many people out on a night like this."

Harkness nodded. "It wouldn't be so bad if I still had the Toms, but they're all working from their flats at the moment with some muscle minding the door if they've got any sense. All frightened off by this Rainlover geezer."

Dwyer lit a cigarette and cupped it inside his left hand. "He doesn't worry you?"

Harkness shrugged. "He isn't after the likes of

me, that's for certain, though how any woman in her right mind can go out at the moment on a night when it's raining beats me." He picked up the evening paper. "Look at this poor bitch he got in the park last night. Peggy Nolan. She's been on the game round here for years. Nice little Irish woman. Fifty if she was a day. Never harmed anyone in her life." He put the paper down angrily. "What about you blokes, anyway? When are you going to do something?"

The voice of the public, worried, frightened and looking for a scapegoat. Dwyer nipped his cigarette and slipped it back into the packet. "We'll get him, Sam. He'll overreach himself. These nut-cases always do."

Which didn't sound very convincing even to himself and Harkness laughed harshly. "And how many more women are going to die before that happens, tell me that?"

His words echoed back to him flatly on the night air as Dwyer moved away into the night. Harkness watched him go, listening to the footsteps fade, and there was only the silence and beyond the pool of light, the darkness seemed to move in towards him. He swallowed hard, fighting back the fear that rose inside, switched on the radio and lit a cigarette.

Joe Dwyer moved through the night at a measured pace, the only sound the echo of his own step between the tall Victorian terraces that pressed in on either side. Occasionally he paused to flash his lamp into a doorway and once he checked the side door of a house which was by day the offices of a grocery wholesaler.

These things he did efficiently because he was a good policeman, but more as a reflex action than anything else. He was cold and the rain trickled down his neck soaking into his shirt and he still had seven hours to go, but he was also feeling rather depressed, mainly because of Harkness. The man was frightened of course, but who wasn't? The trouble was that people saw too much television. They were conditioned to expect their murders to be neatly solved in fifty-two minutes plus advertising time.

He flashed his lamp into the entry called Dob Court a few yards from the end of the street, hardly bothering to pause, then froze. The beam rested on a black leather boot, travelled across stockinged legs, skirt rucked up wantonly, and came to rest on the face of a young woman. The head was turned sideways at an awkward angle in a puddle of water, eyes staring into eternity.

And he wasn't afraid, that was the strange thing. He took a quick step forward, dropping to one knee, and touched her face gently with the back of his hand. It was still warm, which could only mean one thing on a night like this. . . .

He was unable to take his reasoning any further. There was the scrape of a foot on stone. As he started to rise, his helmet was knocked off and he was struck a violent blow on the back of the head. He cried out, falling across the body of the girl, and someone ran along the entry behind him and turned into the street.

He could feel blood, warm and sticky, mingling with the rain as it ran across his face and the darkness moved in on him. He fought it off, breathing deeply, his hand going inside his cape to the two-way radio in his breast pocket.

Even after he had made contact and knew that help was on its way, he held on to consciousness with all his strength, only letting go at the precise moment that the first police car turned the corner at the end of the street.

1

It had started to rain in the late evening, lightly at first, but increasing to a heavy, drenching downpour as darkness fell. A wind that, from the feel of it, came all the way from the North Sea, drove the rain before it across the roofs of the city to rattle against the enormous glass window that stood at one end of Bruno Faulkner's studio.

The studio was a great barn of a room which took up the entire top floor of a five-storey Victorian wool merchant's town house, now converted into flats. Inside a fire burned in a strangely mediaeval fireplace giving the only light, and on a dais against the window four great shapes, Faulkner's latest commission, loomed menacingly.

There was a ring at the door bell and then another.

After a while, an inner door beyond the fireplace opened and Faulkner appeared in shirt and pants, a little dishevelled, for he had been sleeping. He switched on the light and paused by the fire for a moment, mouth widening in a yawn. He was a large, rather fleshy man of thirty whose face carried the habitually arrogant expression of the sort of creative artist who believes that he exists by a kind of divine right. As the bell sounded again he frowned petulantly, moved to the door and opened it.

"All right, all right, I can hear you." He smiled suddenly. "Oh, it's you, Jack."

The elegant young man who leaned against the wall outside, a finger held firmly against the bell push, grinned. "What kept you?"

Faulkner turned and Jack Morgan followed him inside and closed the door. He was about Faulkner's age, but looked younger and wore evening dress, a light overcoat with a velvet collar draped across his shoulders.

He examined Faulkner dispassionately as the other

man helped himself to a cigarette from a silver box
and lit it. "You look bloody awful, Bruno."

"I love you too," Faulkner said and crossed to the
fire.

Morgan looked down at the telephone which stood
on a small coffee table. The receiver was off the hook
and he replaced it casually. "I thought so. I've been
trying to get through for the past couple of hours."

Faulkner shrugged. "I've been working for two
days non-stop. When I finished I took the phone off
the hook and went to bed. What did you want?
Something important?"

"It's Joanna's birthday, or had you forgotten? She
sent me to get you."

"Oh, my God, I had—completely. No chance
that I've missed the party I suppose?"

"I'm afraid not. It's only eight o'clock."

"Pity. I suppose she's collected the usual bunch of
squares." He frowned suddenly. "I haven't even got
her a present."

Morgan produced a slim leather case from one
pocket and threw it across. "Pearl necklace . . .
seventy-five quid. I got it at Humbert's and told
them to put it on your account."

"Bless you, Jack," Faulkner said. "The best fag I ever had."

He walked towards the bedroom door and Morgan turned to examine the figures on the dais. They were life-size, obviously feminine, but in the manner of Henry Moore's early work had no individual identity. They possessed a curious group menace that made him feel decidedly uneasy.

"I see you've added another figure," he said. "I thought you'd decided that three was enough?"

Faulkner shrugged. "When I started five weeks ago I thought one would do and then it started to grow. The damned thing just won't stop."

Morgan moved closer. "It's magnificent, Bruno. The best thing you've ever done."

Faulkner shook his head. "I'm not sure. There's still something missing. A group's got to have balance . . . perfect balance. Maybe it needs another figure."

"Surely not?"

"When it's right, I'll know. I'll feel it and it's not right yet. Still, that can wait. I'd better get dressed."

He went into the bedroom and Morgan lit a cigarette and called to him, "What do you think of the latest Rainlover affair?"

"Don't tell me he's chopped another one? How many is that—four?"

Morgan picked up a newspaper that was lying on a chair by the fire. "Should be in the paper." He leafed through it quickly and shook his head. "No, this is no good. It's yesterday evening's and she wasn't found till nine o'clock."

"Where did it happen?" Faulkner said as he emerged from the bedroom, pulling on a corduroy jacket over a polo neck sweater.

"Not far from Jubilee Park." Morgan looked up and frowned. "Aren't you dressing?"

"What do you call this?"

"You know what I mean."

"Who for, that bunch of stuffed shirts? Not on your life. When Joanna and I got engaged she agreed to take me exactly as I am and this is me, son." He picked up a trenchcoat and draped it over his shoulders. "I know one thing, I need a drink before I can face that lot."

"There isn't time," Morgan said flatly.

"Rubbish. We have to pass The King's Arms don't we? There's always time."

"All right, all right," Morgan said. "I surrender, but just one. Remember that."

Faulkner grinned, looking suddenly young and amiable and quite different. "Scouts' honour. Now let's get moving."

He switched off the light and they went out.

When Faulkner and Morgan entered the saloon bar of The King's Arms it was deserted except for the landlord, Harry Meadows, a genial bearded man in his mid-fifties, who leaned on the bar reading a newspaper. He glanced up, then folded the newspaper and put it down.

" 'Evening, Mr. Faulkner . . . Mr. Morgan."

" 'Evening, Harry," Faulkner said. "Two double brandies."

Morgan cut in quickly. "Better make mine a single, Harry. I'm driving."

Faulkner took out a cigarette and lit it as Meadows gave two glasses a wipe and filled them. "Quiet tonight."

"It's early yet," Morgan said.

Meadows pushed the drinks across. "I won't see many tonight, you mark my words." He turned the newspaper towards them so that they could read the headline *Rainlover strikes again*. "Not with this bastard still on the loose. Every time it rains he's at it. I'd like to know what the bloody police are supposed to be doing."

Faulkner swallowed some of his brandy and looked down at the newspaper. "The Rainlover—I wonder which bright boy dreamed that one up."

"I bet his editor gave him a fifty-pound bonus on the spot."

"He's probably creeping out at night every time it rains and adding to the score personally, just to keep the story going." Faulkner chuckled and emptied his glass.

Meadows shook his head. "It gives me the shakes, I can tell you. I know one thing . . . you won't find many women on the streets tonight."

Behind them the door swung open unexpectedly and a young woman came in. She was perhaps nineteen or twenty and well made with the sort of arrogant boldness about the features that many men like, but which soon turns to coarseness. She wore a black plastic mac, a red mini-skirt and knee-length leather boots. She looked them over coolly, unbuttoning her coat with one hand, then sauntered to the other end of the bar and hoisted herself onto a stool. When she crossed her legs, her skirt slid all the way up to her stocking tops. She took a cheap compact from her bag and started to repair the rain damage on her face.

"There's someone who doesn't give a damn for a start," Faulkner observed.

Morgan grinned. "Perhaps she doesn't read the papers. I wonder what the Rainlover would do to her?"

"I know what I'd like to do to her."

Meadows shook his head. "Her kind of custom I can do without."

Faulkner was immediately interested. "Is she on the game then?"

Meadows shrugged. "What do you think?"

"What the hell, Harry, she needs bread like the rest of us. Live and let live." Faulkner pushed his glass across. "Give her a drink on me and I'll have a re-fill while you're at it."

"As you say, Mr. Faulkner."

He walked to the other end of the bar and spoke to the young woman, who turned, glanced briefly at Faulkner, then nodded. Meadows poured her a large gin and tonic.

Faulkner watched her closely and Morgan tapped him on the shoulder. "Come on now, Bruno. Don't start getting involved. We're late enough as it is."

"You worry too much."

The girl raised her glass and he toasted her back. She made an appealing, rather sexy picture sitting there on the high stool in her mod outfit and he laughed suddenly.

"What's so funny?" Morgan demanded.

"I was just thinking what a sensation there would be if we took her with us."

"To Joanna's party? Sensation isn't the word."

Faulkner grinned. "I can see the look on Aunt Mary's weatherbeaten old face now—the mouth tightening like a dried prune. A delightful thought."

"Forget it, Bruno," Morgan said sharply. "Even you couldn't get away with that."

Faulkner glanced at him, the lazy smile disappearing at once. "Oh, couldn't I?"

Morgan grabbed at his sleeve, but Faulkner pulled away sharply and moved along the bar to the girl. He didn't waste any time in preliminaries.

"All on your own then?"

The girl shrugged. "I'm supposed to be waiting for somebody." She had an accent that was a combination of Liverpool and Irish and not unpleasant.

"Anyone special?"

"My fiancé."

Faulkner chuckled. "Fiancés are only of secondary importance. I should know. I'm one myself."

"Is that a fact?" the girl said.

Her handbag was lying on the bar, a large and ostentatious letter G in one corner bright against the shiny black plastic. Faulkner picked it up and looked at her enquiringly.

"G for . . .?"

"Grace."

"How delightfully apt. Well, G for Grace, my friend and I are going on to a party. It occurred to me that you might like to come with us."

"What kind of a party?"

Faulkner nodded towards Morgan. "Let's put it this way. He's dressed for it, I'm not."

The girl didn't even smile. "Sounds like fun. All right, Harold can do without it tonight. He should have been here at seven-thirty anyway."

"But you weren't here yourself at seven-thirty, were you?"

She frowned in some surprise. "What's that got to do with it?"

"A girl after my own heart." Faulkner took her by

the elbow and moved towards Morgan, who grinned wryly.

"I'm Jack and he's Bruno. He won't have told you that."

She raised an eyebrow. "How did you know?"

"Experience . . . mostly painful."

"We can talk in the car," Faulkner said. "Now let's get moving."

As they turned to the door, it opened and a young man entered, his hands pushed into the pockets of a hip-length tweed coat with a cheap fur collar. He had a narrow white face, long dark hair and a mouth that seemed to be twisted into an expression of perpetual sullenness.

He hesitated, frowning, then looked enquiringly at the girl. "What gives?"

Grace shrugged. "Sorry, Harold, you're too late. I've made other arrangements."

She took a single step forward and he grabbed her arm. "What's the bloody game?"

Faulkner pulled him away with ease. "Hands off, sonny."

Harold turned in blind rage and swung one wild punch that might have done some damage had it ever landed. Faulkner blocked the arm, then grabbed the young man's hand in an aikido grip and forced him to the ground, his face remaining perfectly calm.

"Down you go, there's a good dog."

Grace started to laugh and Harry Meadows came round the bar fast. "That's enough, Mr. Faulkner. That's enough."

Faulkner released him and Harold scrambled to his feet, face twisted with pain, something close to tears in his eyes.

"Go on then, you cow," he shouted. "Get out of it. I never want to see you again."

Grace shrugged. "Suit yourself."

Faulkner took her by the arm and they went out laughing. Morgan turned to Meadows, his face grave. "I'm sorry about that."

Meadows shook his head. "He doesn't change, does he, Mr. Morgan? I don't want to see him in here again—okay?"

Morgan sighed helplessly, turned and went after the others and Meadows gave some attention to Harold, who stood nursing his hand, face twisted with pain and hate.

"You know you did ask for it, lad, but he's a nasty piece of work that one when he gets started.

You're well out of it. Come on, I'll buy you a drink on the house."

"Oh, stuff your drink, you stupid old bastard," Harold said viciously and the door swung behind him as he plunged wildly into the night.

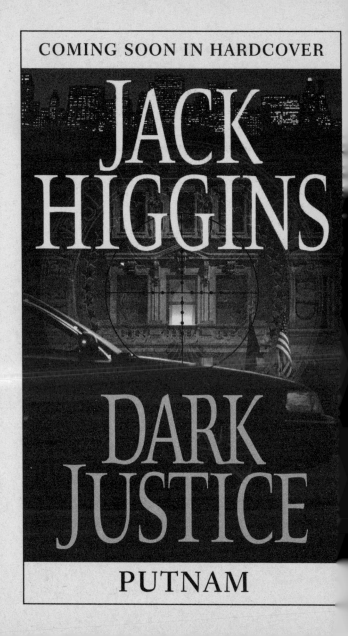